Juliet's Journey to Love

Great Smoky Mountain Getaways

Elsie Davis

Sweet Romance Publishing

Cover Design by getcovers.com

Edited by Elaine Hyatt (Clarity Editing Services) & Cassandra Cornell

Sweet Romance Publishing

Sweetromancepublishing.com

PO Box 778

Liberty, NC 27298

Special Note

JULIET'S JOURNEY TO LOVE was featured in the USA Today Best Seller - A Place to Belong. Other authors included: Melissa Storm, Teri Blake, Carolyne Aarsen, Kristen Ethridge, Heather B Moore, Kat Bishop. Ellie Wade, Rose Castro, Sydney Logan, Laura Ashwood, and Nan O'Berry. Many thanks to all the talented authors who shared this incredible journey with me!

Jeremiah 29:11

"For I know the plans I have for you," declares the Lord, "plans to prosper you and not to harm you, plans to give you hope and a future."

Chapter One

❤

JULIET SHIVERED IN THE dark of night, pulling the sleeping bag up tighter around her neck. Unfortunately, the chill of a cold August evening wasn't her nemesis. Her stomach clenched again, another wave of nausea coming over her unexpectedly. She hoped it was simply a case of last night's dinner not agreeing with her. Unfortunately, she hadn't felt well all day yesterday.

She hadn't said anything to Laura and Blaire, not wanting to alarm them unnecessarily. The Freedom and Faith Women Warriors were a small group of women who met at the First Congressional Church in Memphis. There were five women altogether, but only three of them had been able to make this trip. The group had systematically divided the Appalachian trail into sections with three goals in mind: use the time in nature to grow closer to God, become more independent and strong-willed in life, and, of course, complete the trail.

As the leader of the group, Juliet couldn't afford to get sick. But working as an advanced licensed nurse practitioner in the hospital, she was exposed to a lot of germs, and sometimes, due diligence with washing hands and clothes, and being extremely careful, was simply not enough. Juliet was beginning to think this was one of those times, and the timing couldn't have been worse.

They'd chosen this section of the trail in the Great Smoky Mountains since it was the closest to home and a great way to get a feel for what to expect on some of the longer hikes on the Appalachian Trail. They were two days into the hike, having started from Fontana Dam, and three days away from the pickup location at Newfound Gap, the halfway point of the trail in the Smoky Mountains. Basically, in the middle of nowhere.

Juliet hugged herself tightly and rocked, trying to keep warm. She tried to relax and fall back asleep, hoping whatever was bothering her system would be gone by morning. Judging by her watch, that only gave her an hour or so to recover.

Minutes passed, the oppressive heat inside the sleeping bag becoming unbearable. She rolled over once again, this time unzipping the bag and flinging back the downy comfort. Tiny pinpricks of heat peppered the back of her neck, down her arms, and across her chest. Sweat broke out across her forehead. Using the palm of her hand, she wiped it away. She was burning up, but the cold of the night clung to the sweat and chilled her. It was as though hot and cold were at war within her body and regulating the temperature was a losing battle.

Thirty minutes of tossing and turning didn't help one iota. Instead of feeling better, she felt worse. The pains in her stomach intensified as she clutched her midsection.

Laura got up, disappeared for a few minutes, and then returned. Her friend was big on rising early and getting their morning fire started for breakfast. Juliet remained quiet, not wanting her friend to ask questions. Somehow, she needed to pull it together enough for them to get back on the trail this morning and cover the seven miles intended for today's part of the trail.

It wasn't long before Blaire was up and joined Laura by the fire pit. Laura glanced her way, Juliet scrunching her eyes shut as she tried to delay the inevitable. The sound of footsteps alerted her that it was a losing battle.

"Time to get up, sleepyhead," Laura said, tapping her foot against the bottom of the sleeping bag. "I've got coffee."

Coffee sounded good. And it might just do the trick to settle her stomach. "Thanks, this might be just what I need," Juliet said, trying to sound upbeat as she opened her eyes, sat up and reached for the coffee.

"Don't tell me you're worn out already?" Laura grinned. "We've still got three days and fifteen miles to cover."

"I'll be fine. Just sleepy. Nothing a little caffeine won't cure." Juliet pasted on a smile she wasn't feeling.

"Are you sure you're feeling okay?" Laura's grin slipped into a frown, and she stepped closer. "Your color is a little off."

"It's nothing, I promise. Blaire's cooking might have done me in," Juliet teased.

"Hey, that's not even funny. Those are MRE's. Nobody can screw up ready-to-eat meals," Blaire said defensively, joining in the conversation. "Speaking of eating, our hydrated powdered scrambled eggs and ham are almost finished heating up. We've got thirty minutes before we hit the trail if we're going to stay on schedule."

"I, for one, will be excited to reach our next registered stopping point. More specifically, the extra day we have planned to enjoy the scenic spot. It'll be great if there's others staying at that lean-to and we can trade hiking stories." Laura laughed, moving back to the fireplace and warming her hands.

"Just give me a minute and I'll join you." With her friends occupied by the fire and taking up breakfast, Juliet braved the chilly morning air and crawled out of her sleeping bag. With one arm still wrapped around her belly, she used the other hand to wipe away the fresh beads of sweat on her forehead.

Another wave of nausea hit her. She reached out for the bedpost to steady herself, shooting a quick peek at the others to make sure no one saw or suspected anything. Juliet grabbed her backpack and pulled out a fresh set of undergarments and one of the long-sleeved shirts she'd bought specifically for the hike.

She changed behind the screen they'd hung for privacy, but the actions proved too much in her weakened state. A fresh wave of nausea hit her, only this time it felt different. It was more than a rolling stomach. As she picked up the bag and righted herself, dizziness overcame her. She grabbed the wall for support to keep from falling over.

"Everything okay?" Blaire asked, her gaze swinging toward the lean-to and zeroing in on Juliet. "It's not like you to take a long time to get dressed when it's this cold. Don't tell me you're afraid of my cooking this morning?" she teased.

"I'm...I'm okay. I'm just not feeling myself this morning. I'll be okay in a few minutes," Juliet said, struggling to get the words out, the effort costing her. A fresh wave of pain rocketed across her belly. Pasting a hand over her mouth, she ran past Blaire and Laura and into the woods, searching for some sort of privacy. She leaned back against a tree, doubled over. But nothing she did could stop the contents of her stomach from erupting and spilling onto the ground in front of her. Juliet shook, chills racking her body. Her head pounded in a relentless thumping rhythm.

"Judging by the looks of last night's dinner on the ground, I'd say you're not okay. You look awful," Blaire said dryly, taking her by the arm. "Come on, we need to get you back to bed and figure out what's going on." She reached out to touch Juliet's forehead. "You're burning up with fever. Why didn't you say anything?"

"I was hoping it was nothing," Juliet chattered, grateful for Blaire's support.

"Laura, come quick and help me. Juliet's really sick," Blaire called out.

Laura came running up, helping to support Juliet on the other side. "Let's get her back to bed."

Her two friends led her to the lean-to and helped lay her down, covering her with the sleeping bag.

"What's wrong?" Laura asked.

"I don't know," Juliet groaned. "I've been feeling off since yesterday. I hoped it would pass, but instead, it's worse. I'm sorry."

"Stop. There's nothing to be sorry about. I'm sure you didn't want to get sick. What do you think is going on? You're the nurse here," Blaire asked, reaching out to feel her forehead again.

Juliet fought back another wave of nausea, her body shaking uncontrollably. "It could be anything. Bad food." She tried to shoot Blaire a grin and failed. "Possibly a stomach bug or the flu. There's a lot of that at the hospital I could have picked up."

"What can we do?" Laura asked.

"Maybe some water would help. Cold compress on my head. I don't know." It's not like they had very many options. "I'm sorry. As soon as I shake this, we'll leave. I promise."

"Stop apologizing. By the looks of you, we're not going anywhere. And I'm not taking any chances. Your fever is way too high, something I can tell even without a thermometer. Blaire, stay and keep a close eye on her. I'm gonna take the satellite phone and search out the nearest ridge to try to reach emergency services."

"Sounds good. Just hurry," Blaire said, nodding in agreement.

"Laura, wait. We have a schedule to keep and we can't stop now. I don't want to ruin this for everybody," Juliet said, her teeth chattering in the process.

"Judging by your condition, you're not in a position to stop me. It's for your own good," Laura said, before turning to leave.

Juliet watched as her friend disappeared down the trail. Another epic fail. From failed relationships to failed leadership responsibilities, it didn't seem anything was going to go right in her life.

She wanted marriage and a family, but at the age of thirty, she was finally coming to accept that it wasn't God's plan for her life. Her last relationship, like the two before it, were failures. For as long as she could remember, her parents had been the perfect and loving example of why couples needed to be equally yoked in their walk with God. Most of the people she knew were married with children, or happily close to it, but Juliet simply picked the wrong guys.

Coming to the realization that God's calling wasn't for her to have marital bliss, but to lead and help others, was why she'd accepted the leadership role in the first place. Her family would be a church family. The opportunity had presented itself right after her last breakup, the timing perfect. Now, she wasn't so sure she'd gotten the message right, because this was just one more thing to add to the failure column of her life.

Well, all except for one thing—having smart friends. Juliet knew Laura's decision was the right one because, although she hated to admit it, she was extremely sick.

Juliet rolled over and groaned. Twenty minutes passed and there was still no sign of help. Laura paced the area impatiently, while Blaire busied herself cleaning up the breakfast dishes. Both friends took turns checking on her, applying a cool compress to her head and trying to get her to drink water.

A sound in the distance caught her attention about the same time as the others heard it. The rumblings of a four-wheeler would be her guess. But what if it wasn't who they were expecting? Sick or not, it was her job to keep the others safe.

Juliet reached for her backpack and pulled out the gun she'd packed there. She pushed herself upright using the rail of the bed. She crossed the short distance to join Laura and Blaire at the edge of the woods, hoping to get a better look.

"What are you doing? Are you crazy?" Laura asked, staring down at the gun in Juliet's hand.

She clutched her stomach with one hand and the gun in the other. "N-no. J-just s-safe."

"Oh, for Pete's sake. Who else would be out here when we need them most?" Laura huffed.

"She has a point," Blaire said, shrugging and turning her attention back to the new arrival.

The man driving the ATV skidded to a stop and hopped off the machine. He obviously knew his way around as he started walking the trail toward the creek bridge, the only easy place to cross.

The three of them waited, Laura having fallen silent. The man entered the clearing just as Juliet raised the gun, her hand shaking with the effort.

He looked up as he stepped off the bridge, shock written on his features. Clearly, he wasn't expecting a welcoming committee of four, her gun being the steadfast extra.

"W-who are y-you?" Juliet asked, her voice as shaky as her hand. The man looked more like a bearded hermit than someone here to help. She clutched the gun tighter.

"Someone called in an emergency. And I'm the closest thing you've got to help, Annie Oakley. I suggest you put that thing down before I turn and walk away. Or judging by your color, you pass out." The man's attitude rankled. She considered her effort smart and safe and didn't give a hill of beans what he said. Except, if he was for real, she couldn't risk having him follow through with his threat. She desperately needed help.

"How do we know you're telling the truth? It pays to be careful nowadays," Laura asked, apparently not much liking the look of the guy, either.

Juliet clutched her stomach tighter, fighting back the swimming sea of trees speeding by.

"I'm Jake Kensington. Sheriff Alan Harper sent me to help."

"Sheriff Harper." Laura nodded toward her and Blaire. "He's the one I talked to on the sat phone."

Blaire glanced at the medical bag in his hand and then up at Juliet, her gaze darkening as she took a step toward her. "That's Juliet," she pointed in her direction.

It was all too much. Juliet felt faint, lowering the gun, and putting one hand to her head.

Juliet shook her head, pulling back from the awful odor she recognized. Smelling salt. But why? The fog in her head cleared a tiny bit as she tried to focus.

"Is she okay?" Blaire asked, concern in her voice. "We told her to stay in bed, but she's hard-headed. Please, help her."

"Her pulse is weak, but okay," the man said. The name Jake came to mind, but she didn't know any Jakes.

Juliet tried to pull away.

"It's okay. I'm here to help. I'm going to carry you to your bed and check you over. Do you understand?" He wasn't trying to frighten her any more than she already was, something Juliet appreciated. It's not like she had a choice but to trust him in her condition.

"He's the guy they sent to help, Juliet. It's okay," Laura reassured her.

Juliet shot her friend a quick look and then refocused her attention on the man. She nodded, giving her consent for him to proceed.

Jake picked her up and headed for the lean-to. "Can one of you grab my bag?" he asked, clearly expecting his request to be followed as he walked away. He laid her down on the bed and felt her forehead. "You're burning up."

Tell me something I don't know, mister. The prickly sweat of her skin was driving her nuts. She nodded.

"And judging by the hair plastered to your neck and forehead, you've been running a high fever for a while. First things first, we need to get your fever down. Can someone get me a fresh, cool compress? Stat."

Blaire moved off to get what he needed.

Jake looked up at Laura. "Which one of you called this in?"

"I did," Laura said, nodding.

"Sheriff said you mentioned vomiting. Any more bouts since you called for help?"

"Twice. We've tried to get her to drink water, but she's not had more than a few sips," Laura added, bringing him up to date.

"At first guess, I'm thinking she's got the flu. The fever, sweats, vomiting, and ashen color all fit. The problem is, I can't be sure. And I'm not sure she can keep down a tablet based on what you're telling me." He reached for the cup of water, put a hand behind her back, and lifted her forward. "Try to drink some of this. We've got to get you hydrated."

Juliet noted the compassion in his voice, and it drew forth an unexplained level of trust. Jake wanted to help her—and he cared. She tried, but the effort cost her.

"A couple of sips is a start, but not enough."

"Thank you," Juliet said, her voice soft and weak, barely recognizable to herself.

"Does your stomach hurt?" he asked, lowering her back onto the bed with great gentleness for a giant.

She nodded.

He turned to Laura. "When was the last time she vomited?"

"About ten minutes ago."

"Anyone notice a dark coloring, other than what she might have eaten for dinner last night?"

"No, not that I know of. But then I wasn't exactly examining it." Blaire scrunched up her face in distaste as she handed him the cold compress.

"No," Juliet said, forcing the words from her lips. She would know better than the others.

Jake nodded. If he had any real medical training, he'd know as well as she did that the information was good news. Dark coloring would be indicative of bleeding, and considering the current situation, life threatening.

"Is she gonna be okay? Blaire asked, both her friends hovering close and watching every move Jake made.

"She'll be fine if I have anything to say about it," he said, his voice filled with a confidence Juliet wasn't feeling. He reached into his bag and pulled out a needle. He prepped it before inserting it into an individual dose bottle like those used in the hospital. It wasn't something someone typically had lying around the house. "This is an antibiotic. It's the quickest way to get something into your body to start fighting back. It's critical we get the first dose in you right away. Okay?" he asked, watching her closely.

Juliet nodded. Everything he said made sense to her.

"What's that? Laura asked when he pulled out another vial and combined the contents with the first vial.

"It's anti-nausea medicine. I'm not sure she can hold anything down taken orally," Jake said, trying to put them at ease. Trusting a stranger didn't come easy, but it's not like they had a choice.

Juliet's eyes grew large as he rolled up her shirtsleeve.

"Just a little pick and then hopefully you'll start to feel better. We need to get you to drink some more water. Think you can handle that?" he asked gently, brushing the hair back off her face.

Juliet nodded.

"Good girl." Jake stuck the needle in her arm and injected the fluids slowly. When he finished, he turned to look at her friends. "The sheriff mentioned you all have three more days listed on the plan you registered for this hike. There's no reason you two can't continue, but Juliet's not going anywhere. I'll have to take her back to my cabin and continue to monitor her health. I'm hoping within the next twenty-four hours the fever will break and we'll be on the right side of this nastiness."

"We're not leaving her. If she's going anywhere, we're going with her," Laura spoke up, not happy with Jake's plan of action.

"But what about meeting up with our pickup group at the other end?" Blaire asked, frowning.

"We'll cross that bridge when we get to it. Let's just hope she gets better and then maybe we can make double-time and still make it to the pickup location on time. We'll figure something out. All I know is that we're not leaving her alone with a strange man in the middle of nowhere." Laura was in a take-charge mode, something Juliet was grateful for—even if it was supposed to have been her job.

"Ladies, I'm taking your friend with me, and I'm leaving in five minutes—with you, or without you. I don't care which. So, if you're coming along, I suggest you pack up. Now." It would seem Mr. Gentle had a domineering side when it came to getting his way. He stood, closing his medical bag, and looked down at her. "I've got to get you back across the creek while your friends pack up."

"The sheriff mentioned you had medical training, not that you were a bear. Chill out, Grizzly Adams," Laura said, rolling her eyes at him.

"Name's Jake. Grizzly Jake, if you insist, and I don't give a bear's behind what you think about me. But now, you're down to four minutes." He lifted Juliet into his arms, cradling her against his chest.

His firm chest gave her a sense of security as she inhaled the woodsy scent on his neck. Not a heavy scent, one more like soap instead of cologne. Fitting, considering it didn't appear the man had seen the sharp edge of a razor in years.

"Well, let's just hope, Grizzly Jake, your medical training is more than a two-hour first-aid course," Laura teased. She did, however, start tossing all their things together to comply.

"I reckon my training will do in a pinch. Three minutes," he called out, and started across the bridge.

Juliet's arms slipped around his neck as she held on. "Don't mind them, they're just protective."

"I'm not worried about them. My responsibility is toward you."

Minutes later, her friends had loaded their belongings into the back of the ATV.

"Since we're going to be staying with you, I figure you should get to know us all on first name basis. I'm Blaire, and this is Laura," Blaire said, pointing at Laura. "And you already know Juliet."

Jake nodded. "Great. Now that we've established a first name basis, you need to understand something—my concern is for the patient. You two are on your own."

He settled Juliet across the front seat, propping her upper body across his lap and holding her up with one hand. She felt protected.

"Exactly where are we supposed to ride?" Laura asked, frowning when she realized the ATV was only a two-seater.

"I hadn't planned a group rescue. You can each stand on one side and hang on to the upper bar to keep from falling off. It's the best I can do unless you want to walk." Her friends took his words at face value and stepped up, hanging on for dear life as he put the ATV in gear and shot forward.

Chapter Two

♥

Juliet wasn't surprised when they exited the woods into an open meadow area that revealed a rustic cabin. Given the appearance of her rescuer, it made perfect sense. The man came across as a loner and judging by the appearance of the place, further confirmed her first impression. There were no feminine touches to make the place look homey.

They were both loners, but clearly for different reasons and with different results.

She'd clung to Jake all the way there, as if by doing so, she'd absorb some of his strength. His shoulders were a good indicator he had plenty to share, but as they drew near to the cabin and came to a stop, Juliet tried to move away.

Jake held fast. "Stay put. It's not like you could make it far on your own two feet." He shook his head, his expression clearly mocking her foolish notion to try. He might as well have rolled his eyes and done away with subtlety.

The problem was, he was right. Juliet was too tired to argue—and too smart.

Her friends stepped down off the ATV. Laura made her way to the front door, holding it open for Jake to pass through, Juliet still firmly tucked in his arms.

Jake walked down the hall, which was all of a few steps, confirming her first impression that the place was small. There wasn't much room for four people, much less whoever else lived here. Juliet couldn't help but worry about her friends.

"I'm putting you in my bedroom. It's the only separate room in the place." Which also meant she was putting him out of his own room, for which she felt even more guilty.

"I'm sorry," she said, trying to speak loud enough to be heard.

"Don't worry about it. It's not like you asked to get sick. I'll be right back, but I need to get a few things. Will you be okay?"

Juliet nodded. "My head really hurts. Do you have—"

"I'll take care of it. Save your strength and try to rest. I'll see what I can do for the aches and pains. We've got to get some liquid in you." Jake was in complete control, and Juliet was all too happy to give her care into his efficient hands.

"Okay. I'll try." After Jake left, Juliet glanced around the room, finding nothing to give her a clue about the man or his character. Trusting her instincts had gotten her this far, and she trusted him. Other than the first few gun-pointing seconds when they first met. Those were self-preservation instincts.

A few minutes later, the door opened, and her friends walked in, leaving the door open.

"How are you doing, sweetie?" Blaire asked, soothing back the hair from Juliet's face.

"Not so good. I'm sorry," Juliet said, clutching the blanket up around her shaking body. In minutes, she'd be burning hot again, but at the moment, it was time for the freezing cycle.

"Stop worrying about it. We'll make do for tonight, and hopefully your fever will break and we can be on our way at dawn." Laura's optimism wasn't reflected by Juliet's own impression of the situation.

Having dealt with enough patients as a nurse over the years, she knew her body would be weak after a bout of illness such as the one she was experiencing. "Let's hope you're right," Juliet said, unwilling to be the killjoy. If there was any way to make it happen, she'd walk out of here on her own accord. Sooner versus later.

"But what if she's not better? Grizzly Jake is a loner out here, and he isn't exactly warm and welcoming. Do you know he had the audacity to tell us not to get snoopy around his things?" Blaire huffed. For her normally soft-spoken friend to get upset, Jake must have been exceedingly rude in his warning.

"I don't think he's used to company, if you ask me. He's more than a little rough around the edges," Laura added.

"Sheriff Harper, do you read?" Jake's deep voice had them all turning toward the doorway in an effort to listen.

"Roger that. What's up with the woman?" the newcomer's voice crackled in the living room.

"I think it's a gastrointestinal virus, but it could still be the flu. I'm giving her antibiotic just in case."

"So, it's *not* just a tummy ache?" the sheriff asked.

The three of them looked at each other, none of them sure what he meant. They all kept quiet, interested in hearing more.

"No. If she isn't stabilized and doing better by morning, I'll let you know, and we can get an airlift out here to pick her up."

"You could just drive her into town," the sheriff said.

"I could if the truck was working. But I can't take care of her and fix the clutch, now can I?" Jake's voice had grown frustrated, echoing the sentiments her friends had said about their host.

"Reckon not. What about the other women? Are they continuing on the trail?"

"Unfortunately, no. They're all here at the cabin."

"Really? That ought to be interesting."

"Stow it, Alan. It's bad enough without you adding salt to the wound," Jake said, clearly unhappy with the sheriff and his visitors.

"Roger that, good buddy. Keep me posted."

"Ten-four." Seconds later, Jake appeared at the bedroom doorway.

"What's wrong with her that she might need an airlift?" Blaire asked.

"No privacy with women around, I reckon. Try to not jump to conclusions. It's a precautionary statement if things don't turn around in the next twenty-four hours. Nothing more, nothing less."

"What did the sheriff mean when he said that ought to be interesting having us all here? Should we be worried?" Laura asked, her eyes narrowing slightly as she focused on Jake.

Juliet's friends were looking out for her best interests and it was nice—although it would seem Jake didn't agree.

"I'm not the entertaining kind of guy, in case you haven't figured that out."

"That's an understatement, but don't worry, we'll stay out of your hair. All massive amounts of it. Or at least as much as humanly possible in this tiny place you call home."

"Good, I'm glad we understand each other. Now, I think you two are taxing the patient and would do well to let her rest," Jake said, moving into the room.

"Yes, yes. Of course," Blaire stammered.

"Touchy, touchy. You don't seem like a very happy man. Perhaps you've been alone for far too long," Laura said.

"Lady, you don't know diddly squat about me, and I'd appreciate it if you keep your opinions to yourself."

"Well, your Royal Grizzly Highness, when you get back, can Blaire and I go outside and look around while Juliet is sleeping? Or is that off-limits too?" Laura asked, sarcasm lacing her voice.

"It's a small cabin. Anytime you want to spend outside is fine by me. Just watch out for the bears."

"I think I'd fare better with a grizzly bear over you. Don't worry, Grizzly Jake, you'll have your backwoods cabin all to yourself again soon enough," Laura added.

"Let's hope you don't get a chance to find out for yourself. Around here, they eat people." Jake smirked, and for some odd reason, Juliet's lips twitched, wanting to join in the humor.

"Not much different from you at all then, is it?" Laura retorted.

"I'm not used to company, and it's by choice. What you see is what you get. I keep to myself, and expect you to do the same," he said gruffly. "This cabin isn't made for this many people, so I hope you weren't expecting luxury accommodations. The best I can offer you is the cushions off the couch and a floor for your bed tonight."

"We *are* backpacking the Appalachian trail. I don't know what part of that spells luxury accommodation for you, but you're wrong. Were okay roughing it—trust me. The question is, where do you plan on sleeping?" Laura asked, trying to regain some ground, and put him in his place.

"On the floor. Next to the patient in case she needs me." Jake didn't back down in words or actions.

"I don't think that will be necessary. One of us should be in the room with her," Laura insisted.

"As long as she's in my care, I make the rules. Feel free to camp out next to me." Jake shook his head. "I'll be right back with the pain medication, and I've got to get a bucket in case she throws up again. Unless that is, you all are volunteering for clean-up services?" Juliet's lips twitched with another hint of a smile, even though all the talk was making her head spin.

"Ewww...get the bucket. And hurry," Blaire exclaimed.

Her friends sat down on the edge of the bed and Blaire opened her study Bible and started to read. The words from Psalms brought Juliet a sense of peace, and she let her eyes drift shut.

"This time, I'm serious," Jake said from the doorway, his voice firm.

Juliet opened her eyes reluctantly.

"You all need to vacate the room and let me tend to your friend—without interference." He moved to the side of the bed and waited for them to leave.

"Fine. You don't have to go all he-man on us."

"We're just trying to make her feel better," Blaire offered.

"With a Bible?" he asked derisively, his gaze dropping down to the book Blaire held.

Juliet winced. The readings were soothing, but she wasn't up to trying to explain it to Jake. And his tone of voice was a clear indication he wasn't up to listening, even if she was up to talking.

Her friends left and Jake sat on the edge of the bed. "Here, it's a liquid pain reliever for your headache." He helped her sit up, just like he'd done before, his gentleness an enigma. Juliet managed to get most of it in her mouth, some dribbling down her chin and onto her shirt.

Jake dabbed at the mess with the wet washcloth he'd brought with him. "Good girl. I'm fairly sure you've got the flu or a gastrointestinal virus. Neither one is fun for you, but I'll do what I can to make you comfortable. I plan on another round of antibiotics to be on the safe side at the twelve-hour mark." He used the washcloth to dab at her forehead, brushing her hair back off her face, the cooling sensation a welcome relief.

"Thank you," she murmured, gazing up at Jake. Her eyes glazed over with tears at his tenderness. She brushed at them, not wanting him to make a bigger fuss.

"Do you think you can drink some more water if I help?" he asked. She was grateful he didn't mention her tears.

Juliet nodded. Much to her surprise, she managed to take five or six sips before giving up. It was a good sign, and his look of approval made her more determined to do better next time.

"We'll try again every ten minutes or so, fluids being critical at this point."

"I appreciate you taking me in. I'm sorry if it's a lot of trouble," she said, grateful for his help.

Jake held up his hand. "Say no more. You need to concentrate on getting better. We'll let the medicine do its job, and you get some sleep so that you're doing your job."

"Thank you, Jake," Juliet said, her voice low and still very weak.

He flipped off the light in the room. "Get some sleep, Juliet."

Chapter Three

♥

JULIET BLINKED SEVERAL TIMES, trying to let her eyes adjust to the lighting. Her gaze landed on Jake, who was resting in the chair nearby, and it clicked where she was and why. She'd slept for hours, judging by the time. Throughout the hot and cold changes, she remembered Jake by her side, pressing cold compresses on her face and adjusting her blankets. He'd been quietly attentive in his ministrations.

His eyes opened, and he bolted upright, quickly standing and making his way to her side. "Nice to see you awake again." A smile softened his expression, making him seem more approachable. And handsome.

"Thanks," she croaked. She hated the helpless feeling that assuaged her, much preferring to be the caregiver. Her motto—better to give than re-ceive—had always been a blessing.

"How are you feeling?" he asked, his voice strong and welcoming.

She shrugged. "My stomach still hurts a lot, but I'm not as cold."

"Some improvement is good. Let me get you some more medicine for your stomach. Are you up for drinking some water first?"

"I can try," she murmured, wanting to do well to see the light of approval in his eyes. Jake held the cup to her lips, one arm behind her shoulder. She managed half the glass, which was definitely an improvement.

"Good job," he said, rewarding her with another smile. It wasn't long before Blaire was up and joined Laura by the fire pit. Laura glanced her way, Juliet scrunching her eyes shut as she tried to delay the inevitable. The sound of footsteps alerted her that it was a losing battle.

Jake held the cup to her lips, one arm behind her shoulder.

"Where are Laura and Blaire?" Juliet couldn't help but worry about her friends and how they were faring through this ordeal as she recalled their earlier complaints about Jake and his home.

"They're in the living room. They fixed dinner, which was surprisingly good. But don't tell them I said that—it's easier to keep the status quo that way. And even though I'm a back woods loner, I'm not so out of touch that I didn't have a deck of cards. They've been putting them to good use. I reckon there's not much else here for them to do." Jake's grin confirmed her opinion of the man, but it didn't change the truth of the situation.

"I've ruined the trip for them."

"I think that's the last thing they're worried about. They're concerned about you. You've got some good friends."

"They are, aren't they?" A smile tugged at the corners of her mouth. Juliet was lucky to have them as friends and their quick action may have saved her life. But then, so did Jake's. "I've enjoyed the comfort of your bed, but I was wondering if I could join you all? You know, out in the living room."

"I hardly think you're up to playing cards." He shook his head, nixing her idea without a second thought.

"No. I don't have the energy to play. I thought maybe if I could lay on the sofa, at least then I wouldn't be as lonely and bored to tears. No offense."

"None taken. And I don't see a problem with your request. I'll carry you out there and stoke the fire to provide you with extra warmth."

"That sounds lovely." Not that it mattered what Laura and Blaire thought, Jake was a nice man. Whether *he* wanted to admit it or show it, or not as it appeared.

Jake pulled the comforter from the bed and helped Juliet sit up, wrapping her in the blanket before cradling her in his arms. He carried her out to the front room, Blaire and Laura looking up as he entered.

"Look who's awake," Laura said, smiling.

"It's Sleeping Beauty," Blaire teased. "Are you feeling any better?"

"I wouldn't say better, but definitely not worse. My body hurts. But at least I haven't thrown up again. And I'm not as cold, which is a good sign."

"You would know," Laura said, jumping up to help with the blanket and pillow arrangements as Jake laid her on the couch.

"Are you comfortable?" he asked.

"Yes, thank you. For everything." Juliet reached out to touch his arm.

Jake's gaze drifted to her hand, his brow lines deepening ever so slightly. "Just get better and the three of you can be on your way. That's the best thing you can do for me in return," Jake said, turning away and crossing to the other side of the room where a desk stood in the corner.

Juliet recognized the sudden shift in attitude and realized this was a cold front he erected when the need arose. More like a brick wall. It made her wonder about his story.

"In case you haven't figured it out, Juliet, your knight in shining armor is actually a certified grizzly bear, destined to live out his life alone in his cave," Laura said, chuckling.

Juliet smiled. "Laura, be nice. There's nothing wrong with wanting to live quietly in God's beautiful country." *Nothing wrong with it, but still, an unusual choice.*

"Yes, mother. Or should I say leader," Laura teased.

"Leader?" Jake asked, turning his attention back to her. "I would have thought that role went to you, judging by your pushiness," he said, shooting Laura a smirking grin.

"Ha-ha. Juliet is the leader of the Freedom and Faith Women Warriors', a small group at our church. She organizes the hiking plans and serves as our guide," Laura said, while shuffling the cards.

"I see. And what exactly is the objective of the Freedom and Faith Women Warriors?" Jake asked, his brow tight with deep lines across his forehead.

"A group of women who want to hike the Appalachian trail as an opportunity to get closer to God, fellowship together, and become more independent in our own lives. All while completing the trail as a major accomplishment," Blaire said, summing up the total mission statement for their group, a satisfied look on her face. "There's leftover macaroni and cheese if you get hungry, Juliet. Might be good for your stomach."

"It's my mom's special recipe, minus a few ingredients Grizzly didn't have." Laura's wink was proof her friend was just teasing Jake, something he seemed to take in stride. But then, they didn't know what she knew. He appreciated their cooking.

"No thanks. My stomach is feeling better and I'm afraid to set it off again. This morning was enough. But," she added, stealing a peek at Jake, "I do need to, umm, use the bathroom, if someone will direct me."

Blaire and Laura laughed out loud.

"You do remember where we are, right?" Blaire asked.

"We haven't seen a bathroom since we left the trailhead parking lot. What makes you think Grizzly Jake is going to have anything better than what we've been using the past couple of days?" Laura asked, shaking her head.

"I just thought…"

"You thought wrong," Jake interjected. "First off, I'm not sure you're strong enough to get anywhere on your own and I wouldn't want to take a chance on you falling and injuring yourself. Second, I do have an outhouse, which is slightly better than the woods in my books."

"I'm not letting you carry me to an outhouse." Juliet's face scrunched up in distaste.

"Suit yourself, but I would prefer it if you didn't wait till the middle of the night to tell me you can't hold it anymore. One way or the other, I'm going to have to carry you there. Better during the day. I promise I won't wait inside with you. There's not enough room for two people. There's barely enough for one." He chuckled.

"I'll wait until I feel better." She shook her head. From the standpoint of her bathroom options, it was lucky she hadn't much to drink today; otherwise, she might not have had a choice in the matter.

"Who wants to play cards? We're getting ready to start another game of hearts," Blaire offered.

"Juliet needs to rest. She promised she's only out to watch. And I'll keep an eye on her, but thanks anyway. I'm not into games."

"Suit yourself, Grizzly."

Jake tended the fire, sitting quietly by himself and reading a book in the corner of the room. Juliet found herself curious to know what interested him, but refused to ask, not wanting to delve into his personal life since he was determined to keep them in the dark.

Another hour passed, her friends content to play cards and talk. Juliet grew weary and was more than ready to go back to sleep, except for one little problem. *Make that a big problem.* "Umm, I hate to ask, but I don't think I have a choice. It's not like I'm two-years-old and can get away with wetting my pants. Jake, can you carry me to the outhouse?" The question was dragged from her lips with as much hesitation as humor—the one an attempt to alleviate the other.

"Sure thing." Jake grabbed his jacket to put across her shoulders as he carried her outside. "Your chariot awaits." He winked, his sense of humor making his chivalry bearable.

Chapter Four

♥

WAKING AFTER ANOTHER MID-AFTERNOON nap, Juliet felt better. She brushed the hair back from her face, conscious of Jake sound asleep in the chair not two feet from her. His presence had a calming effect she couldn't begin to understand.

It had been a rough night of tossing and turning in frequent bouts of sweat, interchanged with frequent chills, which had kept her more awake than sleep. But through it all, Jake had been there to tend to her needs. She wasn't quite sure what to make of him yet.

The expression gentle giant came to mind, causing her to smile. His gruff exterior was nothing like the kindness he'd shown her ever since he arrived at their campsite. And then there were his eyes. The warmth in the chocolatey depths not at all like a ferocious grizzly as Laura like to tease him. There was something about Jake that made her want to know more, but unfortunately, they wouldn't be here long enough for her to find out much. The man wasn't exactly an open book.

And other than the one photo of a beautiful woman on the nightstand, there'd been nothing else in the cabin that spoke of people or family. The only vibrant color splashes in the cabin were the striking photographs that hung on the walls. She hadn't missed them when he carried her to the couch and back but didn't dare ask him about anything. He'd mentioned more than once that his personal life was off-limits, something Juliet would respect given that he had taken her in and was nursing her back to health.

And she was certain he'd done just that. Her fever broke this morning, and she felt good—not great, but far better than she had yesterday. Jake had hovered close by, keeping a watch to make sure she didn't overdo things or suffer a relapse. The last thing he wanted was for his house guests to stay any longer than necessary.

It would seem her latest nap had been exactly what she needed. She was well on her way to recovery thanks to good medicine and food. Although, it wasn't like Jake's kitchen was stocked with gourmet food or stocked with much of anything. In fact, she'd bet his medical supplies' inventory far surpassed his food stock. Blaire's cooking skills, however, managed to make everything taste great.

The prayer session they'd held this morning was comforting, her friends continuing to pray for her good health to return and for their ability to finish the trek. They were all anxious to get back on the trail, and if they were going to make it to the pickup location on time, they had to leave in the morning, whether she was ready or not. Juliet felt guilty they wouldn't have the nice relaxing trip and layovers they planned at some of the scenic spots, but there was nothing she could do about the situation.

Jake's offer to fix his truck and drive everyone into town was met with resistance, Laura preferring to finish out their hike. Blaire remained neutral through the discussion.

Juliet couldn't blame her. There was only so much vacation time allocated for hiking all the sections they'd mapped out. Losing this section would be a big deal and force them to do a repeat. And for that reason, Juliet was going to suck it up and make sure she was ready to go in the morning. Jake wasn't happy with the decision, his concern being she could have a relapse and that the final fifteen miles might be her undoing. At least it was better than twenty-three miles.

Once they figured out Jake's place was four miles from the Derrick Knob lean-to they'd camped it, it hadn't taken much to convince her friends to start back in from where the trail picked up by his place. There was no sense in hiking out four miles back to the lean-to, only to return the same way, turning a potential fifteen-mile trek into a twenty-three-mile trek and next to impossible to do. Common sense ruled—at least as far as the Freedom and Faith women were concerned.

Jake, on the other hand, didn't think her urgency to leave or finish the hike had anything to do with common sense. But then he didn't know her or what motivated her. She was the group leader. It was important to finish what she started, and she'd already ruined the trip. She couldn't possibly allow this to turn into a complete failure for her friends.

The leadership role came shortly after her breakup. It made her feel useful. And wanted. And so far, she hadn't been doing a very good job of it.

The bedroom door opened, and Laura and Blaire walked in.

"We didn't know you were awake again." Blaire crossed the room to her side. "How are you feeling? Still okay?"

"With every passing hour, I'm feeling stronger. I promise I'll be ready in the morning."

"Walking from the bedroom to the sofa doesn't prove anything," Jake said from the chair. The sleeping giant had awakened.

"Well, then maybe a walk to the outhouse will do the trick." Juliet smiled as she slid off the bed and stood.

Jake was on his feet in seconds and took a step toward her.

Juliet held up her hand. "I'm fine. Trust me."

"If you say so." Jake stepped back, allowing her to pass. He might have agreed, but she could feel his eyes back, watching her every step.

"She should be okay. Juliet's strong and looking a hundred times better than she did yesterday, thanks to you." Laura's comment made Juliet smile. Her friends seem to have softened her view toward the mountain man.

She took the walk slowly, not wanting the dizziness to return. It was as much of a test for herself as it was a proving ground for the others, and she had no intentions of failing. She reached the outhouse safely, and turned and waved to the others, knowing they'd followed her outside. At least she didn't need Jake to do this for her anymore. Talk about humiliating.

Not that she hadn't appreciated his willingness to do it.

Juliet finished up and started back toward the cabin. A movement off to the side caught her attention, and she stopped to check it out. A small red fox cowered next to the woodpile, the look of pain in his eyes unmistakable. She took a step in his direction and the fox tried to move away, dragging his backside on the ground, obviously hurt.

"Jake," she called with as much energy she could muster.

Jake came running toward her. "What is it? Do you need me to carry you?"

"No." She held out her hand to stop him from picking her up. "Look." She pointed toward the woodpile and the fox. "I think he's injured. He's dragging his back legs when he tried to move, and he looks as if he's in pain. Can you help him?"

"I think you're right. And yes, I'll see what I can do. I'm glad you spotted him. Injured animals don't fare well through the night in the wild. Keep an eye on him for a minute, and I'll be right back."

Blaire and Laura came running toward her. "What is it?" Laura asked.

"Where's Jake off to in such a hurry?" Blaire grabbed her arm.

Juliet pointed toward the fox. "He's hurt."

Jake came back out of the cabin. He was carrying his medical bag in one hand, along with a second larger bag in the other. "Ladies, please stay back. He's still a wild animal and caution is in order." Jake was taking total control of the situation the same way he had when he helped her. They watched as he pulled a small gun from the larger bag and loaded it.

"No!" Juliet hollered, lunging forward to grab his arm, completely disregarding his orders—Laura and Blaire were hot on her heels.

"Jake, you can't shoot the poor fox. That's not helping him," Juliet cried in anguish.

Jake looked down at her arm locked on his, and then at the others as they approached and shook his head. "I told you to stay back. It's not safe. And I'm *not* going to shoot the animal." He glimpsed down at the gun in his hand. "Or at least not the way you think I am. It's a tranquilizer gun. It would be great if you could trust me."

Juliet winced. "I'm sorry, you're right."

The three women linked arms as they stepped back to watch. "He's right. We should trust him, after all, he took good care of Juliet," Blaire said. Laura nodded in agreement.

Jake took aim and fired, the dart landing on the fox's rear flank. Less than a minute later, the fox laid down, his eyes focused on Jake as he approached, and then finally closing. Jake kneeled next to him, checking out the raw, and still bleeding wound.

Juliet broke free from the others, unable to stay back. "Will he be okay? she asked, coming up behind him.

He glanced up at her and frowned. "You don't listen very well. But yes, *she'll* be okay. It looks like the claws of a trap might have torn her leg up or else another animal got the better of her temporarily. Or any number of other things. But I'll take care of it, and she'll be good as new in a few days' time."

"So, are you a vet or a doctor? Because you seem talented in both areas," Juliet asked as she watched him pull out the necessary supplies.

"Neither." Jake wasn't forthcoming with any information, much like before. The man didn't like to talk about himself.

Blaire and Laura had moved forward to stand next to her, the three of them watching as Jake applied some salve to the wound and lightly bandaged it.

"Is she soft?" Blaire asked, wonder in her voice.

Juliet had been wondering the same thing. It wasn't often you got this close to a fox in real life.

"Come and see for yourself. She'll be out for another ten minutes or so. If you keep an eye on her, I'm going to run and get a blanket from the house and set up a makeshift bed for today and tonight. It'll give her a chance to get some rest and start her recovery. She'll have this bandage picked off by then and should be good after that. These types of wounds will normally heal well, and the antibiotic cream should make sure of it."

"Okay." Juliet was the first to kneel, reaching out tentatively at first. "She's not at all what I expected," she said, turning back to the others.

"The fox or Jake?" Laura asked, laughing.

"The fox. Maybe both." Juliet grinned. "But I'm talking about the fox. They look so soft, but the fur is actually course."

"She's beautiful," Laura said, kneeling next to her and reaching out to stroke the animal's back.

Blaire got up the nerve to do the same. "The poor thing. It's almost as if she knew to come here and that Jake would help her."

"I agree. Behind that grizzly appearance, there's a man with a big heart," Juliet said.

"I won't go that far yet, but he's growing on me." Laura laughed.

Jake returned, and the women looked at each other and grinned. That was information they weren't about to share with the man in question. They stepped back out of his way as he lifted the fox into the blanketed box.

Juliet noticed the gentleness with which he laid the animal down. It was the same gentleness he'd used when he carried her. They followed him back to the barn, watching as he set the box inside one of the stalls.

"She'll be safer in here where other animals can't get to her, and it will give me a chance to check in on her throughout the night," Jake said.

"Thank you." Juliet reached out to touch his arm.

With his gaze fixated on her hand, Juliet had the strangest feeling he'd retreated from her, almost as if he were lost in his own world for a few seconds. His gaze shifted back to her, and he nodded. "You're welcome."

"I think this calls for a celebration dinner," Blaire said.

"Not to mention it's a farewell dinner." Laura laughed. "Grizzly man here is finally going to get us out of his hair tomorrow morning."

"Amen to that." Jake grinned. He was a good man with a sense of humor and some incredible healing skills. It reaffirmed her belief that Jake was out here for a reason. Most people just didn't check out and move into a remote cabin. She thought about the picture and wondered if the woman had anything to do with his reasons. It would explain his gruff exterior. If he'd been hurt, her heart went out to Jake. It would take a lot of pain to make someone go to these extremes.

Juliet shoved the thought away, not wanting to ruin the mood. "If you're willing to give prayer thanks for our departure, then you're most certainly capable of joining our prayer session tonight. It would be fun to have you in on the discussion. I think we're talking about forgiveness."

"I'll pass. Praying is not my thing."

"Why not? Maybe it should be. It makes a person feel better inside and can be healing."

"One has to believe, in order for that to work. I don't. End of discussion." Jake was a non-believer, and it was sad because God was exactly who he needed in his life to help him through whatever had caused him to hole away in solitude.

"Well, then. Okay. Message received. But what if you're wrong? Maybe it's something you should think about after we're gone," Juliet said, almost wanting to stay and help him. *The way he helped her.*

"Why don't we see what we can rustle up for dinner and then we can get in a game of hearts before we pack? It'll be an early night tonight," Blaire suggested, trying to ease the awkwardness.

"Yes. And Jake must play tonight since Juliet's playing. We need a fourth for teams."

Jake shook his head. "The food sounds good, but I don't play cards."

"I'll make extra dinners and freeze them for you," Blaire offered.

"Fine, I like food." He shrugged. "Besides, I know you won't stop bugging me until I say yes."

Juliet wasn't so sure those were the only reasons he agreed. Maybe Jake wasn't enjoying his solitude nearly as much as he let on. In a way, the fox and Jake reminded Juliet of herself once upon a time. Lost and hurting, God helped renew her faith and her strength. Life didn't always work out the way one wanted, but for Juliet, her path was to help others.

The fox had Jake for help, but who did Jake have?

Chapter Five

Putting her backpack by the front door, Juliet took a deep breath, willing away the slight shakes it gave her from the effort. Not fully recovered, the weight of her pack was a bit much, but she wouldn't let it stop her. Everything was in motion for them to leave. She'd just keep pounding extra water, snack on protein bars, and keep putting one foot in front of the other. There was no way she was going to let on she was less than one hundred percent. Not even close.

"Is everyone about ready to go?" Laura asked, dropping her backpack next to Juliet's.

Juliet nodded. "I think so."

"Where's Jake? I haven't seen him in a while," Blaire asked, joining the group and adding her backpack to the pile.

"I don't know. He was acting weird this morning. It was like he was reverting back to his antisocial ways." Laura shrugged.

"I think he said something about going out to check on the fox and bringing up the ATV from the barn. Remember, he's taking us to the trail and trying to do everything he can to shorten the trip for me. He's being sweet," Juliet said, defending him. She wanted her friends to see past the gruffness and to focus more on his kindness. They needed to look at his heart. "I'll go check his progress and let him know we're ready to leave."

"You do that. Daylights burning." Laura grinned, eager to be off. But then she had a fiancé waiting for her at the end of the trail. Someone to go home to.

It wasn't that Juliet was against dating and marriage. Her own parents just celebrated their 32nd anniversary and were happily married. It was the fairytale kind of romance Juliet had wanted for herself since she was eighteen. Her dad was a pastor at the church, and her mother, an active member. The love the two of them shared over the years proved how strong the bond could be when two people were equally yoked in holy matrimony.

Which is why Juliet had been determined to do the same—find someone equally yoked in their beliefs. She'd seen what happened when you picked the wrong person. Plenty of her friends in high school had parents who split up, either nonbelievers or unequally yoked. One going to church, one not. One more involved than the other.

In the end, it all added up to the same thing—divorce. Painful splits that ripped apart families. The one that left the deepest mark had ripped her and her best friend apart. She and Sarah had been inseparable, practically from birth. And when Sarah's parents split up, her mother moved to the West Coast, taking Sarah with her. Juliet never saw or heard from her friend again. Best friends torn apart by fate, not of their choosing—and too young to do anything about it.

The split ups were far too like Juliet's own three previous relationships—ones that ended in heartbreak. Her last boyfriend had put on a good act, professing his spirituality on the outside, but on the inside he was empty. It was all a show to get her to date him—and sleep with him. Something she wasn't about to do. When he finally figured out that he couldn't change her mind, the breakup was inevitable. It was for the best, but it didn't stop the hurt that followed.

It was then she began to realize God's plan for her might not include marriage and a family. If her life plan was to serve at the church and to be of help to others as a leader—then so be it. It was why she'd dedicated herself to the Freedom and Faith Women Warriors. The only problem was that it didn't quiet the ache in her heart for a family of her own. But one thing was certain...she would trust in God for the answers. It was the only way her heart would know peace.

Heading for the barn, she went in search of Jake, stopping at the stall where he'd put the fox. Curled up in a ball, the fox was asleep, more than likely still a little groggy. Juliet rounded the corner and spotted Jake leaning against the ATV, one hand on the support bar. It was an odd position, considering he wasn't doing anything but standing there. He reached up and wiped his brow with the sleeve of his shirt.

Juliet didn't say a word, intuition telling her to watch. Jake was a man with a purpose in everything he did, and right now, he was acting strangely. He wiped his forehead again. Enough is enough—Juliet wanted to know what was going on.

"Jake, what's wrong?"

He shot a quick look in her direction before letting go of the bar. "Nothing. I'm just checking on the ATV." He didn't look fine. His coloring was off. Suddenly, it clicked. Jake had caught the virus from her.

She shook her head. "I wouldn't say it's nothing, considering you're not doing much of anything right now. Do you feel all right? Maybe you caught the virus." There was no maybe about it, and knowing Jake was sick changed everything.

Jake looked away, sliding into the driver's seat, and starting the engine. "I said I'm fine," he snapped. "Is everyone ready to go? I need to get you to the trailhead so I can get back and check on the fox again. She's starting to move around more, and I'd like to keep an eye on her." Every word he said seemed to come with effort.

"They're ready, but I'm not. And the fox is sound asleep at the moment." Juliet knew she was right. The signs were all there, and as a nurse, she couldn't overlook them. Jake was going to need help and Juliet couldn't leave him alone. This was a disaster. It was important for her to lead the women back to the pickup location and to finish the hike with them, but it was more important for her to help Jake the way he helped her.

"Hop in; I'll drive up front." Jake leaned against the steering wheel as he waited for her to climb inside. "Why aren't you ready to go?"

"Because I'm not leaving you." It was the right answer, whether Jake liked it or not.

"I don't want or need you here. I'm fine," Jake said stubbornly.

"It's not like you're in a position to make me leave. So quit arguing. I'll run the others to the trailhead. You, on the other hand, need to get into bed," Juliet said just as Jake pulled up in front of the cabin.

"Bossy much?" He shook his head.

"When I need to be."

"Well then, it's a good thing you're not my boss."

Laura and Blaire came out carrying all three backpacks. "We were wondering what kept you guys so long. Is the fox okay?" Blaire asked, looking back and forth between the two of them.

"The fox is doing great, but the plan has changed. Jake caught the virus and I'm not leaving him alone. I'll drive you as far as the trailhead, if you two think you can manage the rest of the hike without me," Juliet said, disregarding Jake's comment.

"Wow. It's not a major surprise. I guess we should have seen this coming, considering he was in close contact with you. But I don't like the idea of you staying here alone with him, sick or otherwise," Laura said. "Doesn't seem right."

"This isn't the dark ages. I'm a grown woman and I'll be fine. But what about you two?"

"You may be the group leader, but you're not the only Girl Scout in town." Laura grinned.

"Point taken. You've been as much a lead in this as I have, probably more, considering I got sick," Juliet said, shaking her head. The whole trip had turned into a fiasco because of her illness. If she finished the trip with her friends, it would go a long way to salvaging her pride—but pride didn't count when duty called. But she couldn't help the resentment growing in her heart, knowing Jake didn't want her here. Rejection was something she should be used to by now, but it didn't take the sting away.

"I still don't like the idea of leaving you."

"Ladies, none of you are staying. End of discussion. Can we go?" Jake spoke up, desperation in his voice. He swiped at his forehead with his sleeve again.

"You're not calling the shots on this one, Jake. Sorry." Juliet turned to Laura. "If it'll make you feel any better, put a call into the sheriff and get him to vouch for Jake. I already trust him, so it's for your benefit."

"That sounds like a plan." Blaire nodded. They all headed inside, leaving Jake to follow. He wouldn't want them using the CB radio without his oversight and it was a surefire way to get him inside—and one step closer to bed.

"Anyone know how to use this thing?" Blaire asked.

"Press the button on the side and talk," Jake said, clearly resigned the women were going to do exactly as they wanted. Which was true.

"What do I say?" Blaire asked, looking unsure of herself.

"How would I know? Just talk. They won't care if you're not using CB jargon," Jake said, shaking his head and leaning against the wall for support. "I thought I was going to be free from you all." Another affirmation he wasn't feeling well, and they didn't have long before he'd be down for the count.

Juliet tried to recall how quickly it had set in with her.

"Sheriff Harper. Come in, please, Sheriff Harper. Hello?" Blaire tapped the mic and looked up at them. "Nothing. He's not answering."

"That's because you've got to take your finger off the button after you speak," Jake said, his patience wearing thin.

"Oh." Blaire released the button and waited.

"Sheriff Harper. Who is this?" the man on the other end asked.

"Blaire Livingston. My friends and I have been staying at Jake's cabin for the past two days. Juliet was sick, and he came to help us, but now he's got the virus. She wants to stay here with him. He's not, ummm, like a bad person to leave her with, right?"

Jake let out a grumbling sound and crossed the room, taking the mic out of Blaire's hand. "Alan, she wants to know if her friend's virtue is safe with me or if I'm going to murder her in her sleep." He glared at Blaire and Laura. "Sometimes being direct is a lot more effective, and if it will expedite getting you out of here, it works for me."

"By the sounds of it, he's going to be too sick to do anything about anything, not that he would. You have nothing to worry about. Man's a certified loner these days. Jake, it sounds like you need a good doctor. Know of one?" The sheriff chortled before he was cut off.

Juliet grabbed the mic from Jake. She held it up to her mouth and pressed the button. "This is Juliet. He doesn't need a doctor—he's got a nurse. Me. I'm staying, whether he likes it or not."

Jake scowled.

"That's even better," the sheriff answered. "Jake, you got your hands full, buddy, but they sound like capable hands. I'm off. Ten-four, over and out."

Juliet didn't miss the Sheriff's "these days" comment. Another clue she was right about Jake. He wasn't always the way he was now. Although, at this minute, none of it mattered. Getting him to bed did. The man was pale and hanging on to the desk for support. She could see him getting worse by the minute, and it was an all too familiar pattern of what she'd experienced.

"You." She poked Jake in the chest. "Get. Into. Bed. Now." Juliet turned to her friends. "Let's get a move on. Pretty soon, I won't be able to leave him, so it's now or never for me to get you back to the trailhead."

"Woohoo! Take-charge Juliet is back in action." Laura laughed. "I'm satisfied you'll be okay, and I'm ready if Blaire is."

"Ready," Blaire added, making a beeline for the door.

"If you're not in bed by the time I return, mister, I'm going to put you there myself while I still can." Juliet wasn't about to let Grizzly Jake win this battle.

Chapter Six

♥

JULIET PULLED UP TO the trailhead and parked. Laura and Blaire loaded their gear on their backs, before stepping close to give her a hug.

"Be safe, you two," Juliet said, her emotions still conflicted about leaving. It would have been nice to finish the trek, but staying was the right thing to do. She owed Jake big time. And even if she didn't, she would stay. Her medical training and her heart for others wouldn't allow anything less.

"You too," they said in unison.

"Don't let Grizzly Jake boss you around too much. By the time you get back, he'll be more like a teddy bear I reckon." Laura laughed.

"That I'd like to see," Blaire added, grinning. She adjusted the straps on her pack.

"Get going. Day's a wasting," Juliet said, knowing she needed to get back to Jake regardless of his bear status.

Her friends started down the trail to continue the hike, turning to wave as they rounded the bend that would take them out of her line of sight. "Please, Lord, keep them safe."

Juliet slid back into the ATV and headed for the cabin. As she pulled up in front of the place and headed inside, it took her less than sixty seconds to realize Jake wasn't there. The obstinate man clearly hadn't followed any of her instructions.

"Jake!" she hollered, stepping out onto the front porch. He didn't answer, her fear for him ramping up into overload. She had to find him. Juliet raced for the barn and it didn't take her long to find the object of her search.

Fixing his truck...of all the lame-brain things he could be doing. "There you are. Why didn't you answer me? What are you doing out here? I thought I told you to get into bed. Typical male. You don't listen," she prattled on, shaking her head in frustration.

"Typical woman. I can't get a word in edge wise to answer. I need your help," Jake said, not sounding at all like himself.

Juliet's mouth formed an o, her eyes wide in surprise. She rushed to his side. "What's wrong? Is it the virus?"

"Yes. I hate to admit it, but you were right. Don't think I can get back to the cabin without you." His face was ashen, and it appeared to take a great amount of effort just to stand on his own two feet as he used one hand to support himself on the truck.

"Here," she said, taking his free arm and laid it over her shoulder. "I'll do the best I can. Try to help as much as you can manage."

"What? No *I told you so*?" he asked, forcing the words out as if it were an effort.

"Hardly. I'm a professional. It doesn't matter what you did or didn't do; what matters is that we deal with what we have now. Let's get a move on, Grizzly." She smirked.

He cocked an eyebrow in her direction. "Fine. I'm in no position to say anything otherwise." Jake was trying to not put all his weight on her, but with each step, the pressure increased.

It wasn't far now. Jake stumbled and Juliet's free hand came up to catch him around the chest, steadying him. "Easy. Let's take this slow and steady," she said, hoping to encourage him that they could make it the rest of the way and he wouldn't be stuck out in the front yard for the night.

Jake wiped his brow and stopped to clutch his stomach as a wave washed over him again. "Sorry."

"Better now? Five more steps and we're inside, and I will get you straight to bed."

Jake nodded.

The two of them barely fit side-by-side as she helped him down the short hall to his room. "Just lay back and I'll get you a cold compress, and then I'll get your boots off so you can get comfortable. Is your medical bag in the kitchen? I can get you some of the nausea medicine and the pain relievers."

"I think I can manage my own boots. But yes, the bag is in the kitchen. If you bring it to me, I can do my own injections."

"Or you can let me do it so there's no mistakes. I'd lose my license if I let a patient administer their own injection voluntarily."

"I'm not your patient."

"I beg to differ. I did just put you to bed." Juliet winked. The humor was lost on Jake as he started to shake, and she hurried out of the room to get the supplies and return with a fresh blanket.

Juliet was back in short order, and it didn't take long to realize that once again, Jake had ignored her orders. Or tried to ignore her orders. A slight smile tugged at the corners of her mouth, but she didn't say a word as she took over the act of boot removal, something he was failing at miserably.

Jake stopped fighting the inevitable and lay back, letting Juliet have her way.

Boots off, she proceeded to give him the shots, repeating the process he'd done with her. She used a cold compress to wipe his brow.

"I'm not a child, you know," Jake muttered.

"Then quit acting like one. It's called being sick. And sometimes, that means needing a helping hand."

A wave of nausea hit Jake as he doubled forward, clutching his stomach.

"Let me get the bucket. Like you, I don't relish the idea of cleaning up vomit."

"Nice to know you have your limits," Jake said, laying back against the pillows. "My limits are not having you in the room if I *do* vomit."

"I've seen people throw up before, trust me. It's no big deal."

"It's a big deal—to me. Please." Jake had reduced to begging in an attempt to salvage his pride and it tugged at Juliet's heart. The man was stubborn, just like her father. But that's where the similarities ended.

She nodded. "We'll compromise. I'll get you the bucket and leave you alone if it looks like you're going to throw up. Otherwise, I get to sit here and watch you sleep. And when you're awake, I'll keep you company. Deal?"

"Deal."

"Oh, and one other thing. What do I do with the fox?"

"When she's up and active, you can open the door and let her out. She'll take her time and instinct will take over."

"Got it. Something else I can manage, so don't worry." Juliet left the room in search of a bucket.

The truth was, Jake was more like her father than she cared to admit. He was kind and generous, although sympathetic with animals instead of people, but he was a good man. She returned to the room minutes later, bucket and Bible in hand.

"This is for when you're sleeping." She held up her study Bible when she noted the questioning look in his eyes and slight scowl. "It's my Bible studies and I've got a few days' worth of catching up on my daily reading to do. I'd be more than happy to share it with you if you're interested."

"I'm not."

Any response she might have tried was waylaid when Jake succumbed to another round of shaking and stomach pain. His face was ghostly white, her signal to leave the room and let him do his business without her watching on.

Juliet looked up from her Bible, gazing at Jake as he slept. She knew the medicine would help but sleep, more than anything, would get them through it. That, and plenty of water. She'd already refilled his glass for the next time he woke up.

After she had returned, Juliet had turned out the lights to darken the room, using only a lantern as a dim light to read. It was then she had time to focus on the woman's picture on the dresser, and it left Juliet wondering again about Jake's story. She was certain the woman had something to do with the pain she saw reflected in his eyes, always just on the surface, but hidden unless you were looking carefully.

It was odd sitting in his bedroom, being the one to watch over him. At the hospital with patients, it was different. The sterile environment made it easy for things to stay impersonal. But there was nothing impersonal about being in Jake's bedroom. Pulling off a man's boots had been a first for Juliet. It was so personal. She knew without a doubt Jake wasn't feeling well at all for him to allow her to do the things she was doing. And yes, she could gloat about it, but she'd been honest. What good would that do? There was no sense in pushing him harder to fight against the inevitable.

Juliet thought back to when she found him in the barn. She hadn't missed the blue tarp that had been drawn off the truck, and she instinctively knew he'd gone out to fix the clutch. His determination to get rid of her had superseded his own health. Jake wanted her gone, that much was obvious—but he had nothing to worry about from her. It's not like she'd be setting her sights on him—no matter how nice he could be at times.

Although, nice at this point was a stretch. Except there was something about him that went beyond the bearded, gruff exterior. Something she didn't quite understand.

Was it possible God had placed her in Jake's life for a reason? How much help could she give a person in two days, especially given he was sick? Perhaps she was reading too much into the situation, and it was just a matter of coincidence. Nothing more than the fact she was here to help him get better. But then, if she hadn't shown up in the first place, he wouldn't be sick.

Juliet got up to wipe Jake's brow in an effort to cool him as he began to toss and turn.

His eyes fluttered open.

"Hey there. How are you doing?" Juliet asked.

"I feel like I've been hit by a freight train," Jake said, his voice raspy and strained.

"Here, drink some water," she said, keeping her voice soft . Juliet had learned quickly that the gentle approach netted far better results with patients. She reached behind his back and helped him sit up, lifting the cup to his lips. It must have cost him great effort not to say anything about her assistance.

He finished half a glass, much to her satisfaction. "Thanks," he whispered.

She helped him lay back against the pillows. "Do you need me to help you to the bathroom?" She couldn't help but grin, remembering the problem she herself had faced two days ago.

"No," Jake said a little more forcefully, shaking his head for emphasis. The man had his limits.

"Would you like me to read to you?"

"No. If you insist on babysitting, then tell me about yourself."

A one-sided conversation would be awkward. Besides, how much was there to really tell? "I can do that. Oh, but first, you'll be interested to know our fox has returned to the wild, just as you said she would. It was kind of a special moment—knowing we helped."

"Good, very good," he said, a smidgeon of tension draining from his firm jaw.

"As to my life, I promise you it's not interesting, but then, maybe my story will help you fall back asleep." She grinned.

Jake attempted a smile, failing miserably. But it was the effort that counted in her book.

"My whole name is Juliet Anne Walker, and as you already know, I'm an APRN. I live in Memphis, although I'm originally from Dylan, a small bedroom community just outside of Memphis. My father's a pastor there, and he and my mother have been married for thirty-two years. Happily, I might add. The job offer came in after I graduated from the College of Nursing at the University of Tennessee in

Knoxville. Back then, I saw it as an opportunity to break away from the parents and go out on my own." She shrugged.

"It was good at first. City life and all, but I'm not sure it's me. I miss the small community aspects of Dylan, a place where everyone knows your name. Don't get me wrong, I love my job, but sometimes, I keep wondering if there's more I should or could be doing. Are you sufficiently bored yet?"

"Keep talking. I'll let you know when to stop. Either that, or I'll fall asleep." Juliet could have sworn there was a hint of a smile with his words.

"This is just awkward. I'd be more comfortable reading from my study book. What do you have against me reading to you? It would be far more interesting."

Jake flicked a glance at the photo on his nightstand, the move more telling than Juliet could have imagined. "Religion is not my thing. Surefire way to put me to sleep."

"Fine. I'll tell you a bit more and then I'll read. Like you said, it'll put you back to sleep, which is what you need to help get through this. And while you sleep, I'll try to fix something for you to eat when you wake up. Maybe some chicken soup and crackers."

Jake rolled his eyes but didn't say a word.

Juliet took that as an agreement, more than happy to reach out and share a little of God's love with. "More about me. Let's see, I've been at the hospital for five years now. I work in the clinic section, dealing with patients who comes in for urgent care, but it keeps me out of the emergency department and the intense stuff. I like the idea of sleeping at night." She smiled.

"You didn't mention a husband or boyfriend waiting for you back home. Surely, you're not an all-work and no-play kind of woman?" Jake said, his gaze never leaving her face.

Juliet was surprised he made the effort to talk to her. For that, she decided to reward him with the truth. "No husband. No boyfriend, for that matter. Last one parted way with me about two months ago."

"Why?" he asked, frowning.

"I know you're not big into God's word and the wisdom that comes with it, but it's the only way I can explain the why, so you'll have to bear with me.

Watching my mother and father happily in love for all these years made me want what they have. They both were Christians when they met and married. My father became a pastor and my mother has lovingly helped at the church and leads some of the women's groups—always by his side. The two share everything together. It's beautiful. The Bible mentions people being equally yoked with one another with regards to matrimony. It's what I want."

"Sounds like they both have egg on their face." Jake grinned, his attempt at humor oddly satisfying given his condition.

"Wise guy. I think you know differently and the truth. When I was younger, friends' parents would get divorced, or relationships broke up, leaving a trail of broken hearts. One thing I noticed was that couples who were unequally yoked rarely survived. When my best friend'sparents divorced, Sarah was ripped away from everything she knew to move far away with her mother. Including me. I've never seen or heard from her again. People need to be in a relationship with people that have similar beliefs in God, Jesus, and in their walk of spirituality." She'd never explained her feelings to anyone before, but at least with Jake, it's not like she'd ever see him again or that he really cared. Her secret was safe.

"Sounds like an easy way to walk away from a relationship, if you ask me."

"I don't agree. I want one that'll last forever, not a couple of years, or worse, a couple of months. Besides, it's not like you have the voice of experience to back up your statement."

"That's not entirely true. I was married once, and we weren't on the same page when it came to religion. But I loved my wife whole-heartedly." The catch in Jake's voice gave her pause, urging her to try and help him manage the ache in his heart. She had a feeling he didn't talk about his past, and that he had unknowingly just revealed the source of his pain.

"What happened?" Juliet couldn't believe Jake was sharing this information with her. Perhaps the medication had loosened his resolve and determination to remain aloof. Perhaps the virus had done what no one else had done—wear him down.

"She died. End of discussion. I'm tired." His words came as a shock and Juliet knew when to back off and this was definitely the time.

"Okay. I'll read a bit until you're asleep. Then I'll fix you some dinner. That way, when you wake up, it'll be waiting."

Jake rolled over, not bothering to answer.

Aloof was back in place.

Chapter Seven

♥

JULIET WENT OUTSIDE TO gather some flowers to put in a basket, hoping color would bring the cabin to life. Her gaze automatically drifted to the tree line in hopes of seeing the fox again, but there was no sign of her. When she spotted some of the truck parts and tools lying on the ground, she took the time to pick everything up before heading back to the house. Of course, she also took the time to stop and appreciate Jake's truck—a 1940 Ford. It was in rough shape, but still a classic.

Last night, Jake had missed dinner, and the night had been rough. His fever seemed to have broken around one a.m., but he'd tossed and turned long after that. Breakfast was more like toast and coffee, and he needed to eat a better lunch.

Returning to the cabin, she walked through the front door, immediately spotting Jake sitting on the couch. "Just couldn't stay in bed, could you?" She smiled, putting the basket of flowers on the table.

"You're not my mother, and I don't need permission." Jake smiled. It softened the gruff exterior he presented to the world. His disposition was a clear indicator of how much better he was doing, especially given he was up and about.

"Good thing for you, or you'd have been grounded six times over. You don't follow directions very well." She laughed. "Is there anything I can get you?"

"No, thank you. You've been amazing. Even if I hadn't known you're a nurse, it would've been my first guess. You have an incredible bedside manner."

"Why thank you, kind sir. I can't believe how quickly you're recovering."

"It could be the virus strain gets weakened as it's passed from person to person. But then there's also the fact that I'm a lot taller and heavier than you are."

"I think you look great," she said, blushing to her root. Her professionalism had clearly gone out the window. "I mean, I think you're right."

"Thanks. Nice to know we agree on something. The right part." He winked. Jake was doing his best to look like he was recovered, but to Juliet's trained eye, he still looked weak. Certainly not the overpowering presence she'd come to expect.

"Lunch will be ready in about thirty minutes. You think you can eat something?" Juliet headed for the kitchen, pausing at the entrance to turn and wait for his answer.

"A small plate would be great. Whatever you're cooking smells delicious and definitely has me thinking about food again."

"That's awesome. Do you want to play cards until it's ready?"

"Maybe later this afternoon. There's something else I'd like to talk to you about."

His easy response was surprising. "Okay. Hang on and I'll be right back." She couldn't help the curiosity that consumed her as she wondered what he had to say. She checked on the casserole baking in the oven and then returned to join Jake.

"Come sit down," he said, patting a space on the sofa next to him.

The move was totally out of character. "Now you've really got me curious." She crossed the room and sat in the chair next to him instead.

"I don't bite," he said, glancing at the spot at the other end of the sofa and then back at her.

"That's not what I heard. Laura thinks you're all grizzly bear."

"Maybe I'm one of the nice bears. Like Yogi."

"Maybe, but I think I'll play it safe and stay here." She shrugged. "So, what you want to talk to me about?"

"I got an email today from someone in town. They—"

Juliet held up her hand. "Wait, what? How did you get an email here?" she asked.

"I have a sat phone, and it's connected to the internet." Jake acted as though it were information she should already know.

"And you didn't think to tell me? What if I had needed to reach somebody when you were sick? Not a smart move, mister."

"No one asked. And you all were enjoying your woodsy experience, and I didn't want to ruin it for you," he teased.

Juliet picked up the pillow on the chair and threw it at him. "Thanks a lot."

Jake caught the pillow and set it aside. "Nice shot. But as I was saying, I got an email that said the doctor in Hollow Creek left town. Seems he took a city job in New York and just walked out, leaving the clinic without a medical professional to tend to patients. The town has no one right now and the closest medical office is over fifty miles away."

"That's terrible. If any emergency arises, there's no one to help them."

"Exactly. I got to thinking about what you said about your job and city life and looking for a change. Why don't you apply for the job?" Nothing he could have said would surprise her more. Jake was trying to get her to stay in Hollow Creek. Of course, it was her nursing skills that prompted the suggestion and not her.

"I'm sure they'll be looking for a doctor…something I'm not," Juliet said, knowing it was true. Every clinic had to have a doctor in charge.

"Hollow Creek is a small town and just inside the Tennessee border, so your license is valid to practice. I reckon they'd be thrilled to have you, doctorate or otherwise." Jake was pressing her to apply, but he didn't understand the way things worked.

The idea was tempting, but not realistic. "I don't know. It would completely uproot my life." She needed to derail his train of thought, but the words wouldn't come out. It was nice to consider the possibilities, even if only for a short while.

"But you said you were looking for change, and that you wanted to shake things up in your life. Now's your chance."

"That it would. I don't know. It's not that easy of a decision." Especially considering she had a lucrative job back in the city, even if she didn't enjoy it as much as she once did. She loved nursing and helping others, but the endless sea of nameless faces grew tiring. A small community would be amazing. But was it sane?

Jake stood and crossed the room in silence. When he turned back to face her, his expression was filled with determination. "I think you'd be perfect for the clinic. Make it conditional and tell them it's only temporary. It would give you a chance to see what you think. It would be a win-win for you and the town, as it would help tide them over until they found someone else."

"Too bad you weren't doing the hiring," Juliet said, laughing. Jake had a way of making it sound like an opportunity she'd be crazy to let pass.

"I'm sure anyone who met you would love you. I mean, love what you bring to the table," Jake stuttered.

"Wow. Grizzly Jake paying a compliment. I'm impressed. Maybe it's time I started calling you Jake."

"I would consider it an honor." He grinned, shooting her a wink.

This was a fun, teasing side of Jake, one she was having trouble adjusting to. Even his gruffy beard and shaggy hair were growing on her. And if Jake was coming out of his shell, what did it mean in terms of him embracing life and letting go of the pain that held him trapped here in the cabin?

More and more, Juliet played with the idea God must have sent her to Hollow Creek with a purpose. A purpose that was starting to look as if it included the town—and Jake.

Staying here would give her the chance to focus on others instead of her own shortcomings—like failed relationships and failed leadership duties. Maybe this was something she could get right. "You know what? I think I will apply." She nodded, growing stronger in the decision. It's not like it meant she would get the job.

It would be weeks before she even heard, which would give her a chance to really think over such a major life change and figure out if she could make it work. Then there was the time needed to talk to her boss about a short leave of absence. A temporary trial period sounded heavenly, even if just for a change in her daily routine. Maybe it was what she needed to rediscover her joy of nursing.

"Since you're feeling better, do you think perhaps you can drop me in town? I'll stop in at the medical center to put in an application." If it's meant to be, she'd get the job. If not, then she'd wait for God's plan to reveal what's next in her life.

"That's great." Jake beamed. "There's only one problem."

"What's that?" she asked.

"The truck's not working yet. My attempts to fix it yesterday were, umm…delayed."

"Maybe later we can work on it together," Juliet offered.

"We?" he asked, coming to stand next to her.

"We. I know a thing or two about engines. Including the old 1940's classic Fords," she added for good measure. Juliet had been one of the two women brave enough to take shop class with the other guys in high school. Turned out to be a blessing more than once when her old car stopped working.

"You continue to surprise me at every turn."

"Good. There's more in store where that came from." Juliet found herself praying she did get the job, if for no other reason than to see more of Jake. To help him, of course. Because she couldn't forget, no matter how genuine and kind he was, they weren't equally yoked and therefore, nothing could ever come of any attraction that stirred up to life. Not that a part of her wasn't interested in finding out.

Chapter Eight

♥

"**J**AKE, LUNCH," JULIET CALLED out, putting lunch on the table.

He didn't answer. She went to find him, only to discover he wasn't in the cabin—which left the outhouse or the barn. She'd lay bets the man was in the barn working on the truck.

Without her.

"Lunch is ready. I thought you were going to let me help you," she said, walking into the barn to discover him bent over the engine.

"I hadn't realized you were serious about helping," Jake said, tossing a wrench in the toolbox. "Let me just get this last piece off and then I'll be ready to drop in the new clutch. After that, it might be nice to have a second set of hands to help hold the parts in place while I put the starter and the transmission back in."

"Not a problem. The clutch is always in a tough spot, it seems. I don't know why they can't design engines that we can get to everything easily. My dad would love this vintage truck. He's usually got one in the garage that he's working on. I think the current project is an old Chevy. He restores and sells them."

"Sounds like a great hobby."

"It is. Maybe the secret to a happy marriage is having great hobbies, not just being equally yoked," Juliet said, laughing.

"That sounds more reasonable to me," Jake said. He removed the last of the nuts and pulled the old clutch out, tossing it on the tarp. "Let's eat."

They walk side-by-side back to the cabin. Jake made a beeline for the sink and started to scrub the grease off his hands. Using some of the orange degreaser popular with mechanics, he finished in no time.

Moving to the table, they sat down next to each other. Juliet looked up at him and smiled. She reached out to touch his face. "You have a spot of grease you missed." Using her napkin, she wiped at his forehead.

"Now you know why I have a beard. I'm sure there's more in there I've missed." Jake used his own napkin and wiped at his beard in its entirety.

"Do you ever shave it off?" she asked, curious why anyone would want to have that much hair on their face all the time.

He grinned. "Nope. I trim it occasionally, but don't see the reason to go to the trouble of cutting it. It'll just grow back again."

"I see." She didn't, and it made her wonder all that much more. "Not hiding behind it, are you?"

"Hiding from what?"

She shrugged, deciding to test his limits. "Yourself maybe."

"Don't go there, Juliet," Jake said, tossing his napkin back on the table.

She took his hand in hers, surprised when he looked down at where their hands were joined, but didn't pull away. Instead, he looked at her, a question in his gaze.

"Father God, we thank you for this glorious day and thank you for the food we are about to receive for the nourishment of our bodies. Thank you for bringing Jake into my life, and for the blessing he was in helping me to get healthy. In Jesus' almighty name we pray, Amen."

She squeezed his hand one last time before she let go and picked up her fork to start eating. "I know you don't want to talk about your personal life, but you mentioned your wife died. I wonder if that's why you live out here now. I like you, Jake. And I would just like to understand you more—to be a blessing to you."

"To be a blessing to me would be not to pry."

"It's not prying, it's helping someone in need."

"Let's agree to disagree." Jake wolfed down his lunch in silence. Scooting back in his chair, he took his plate to the sink to rinse it off and set it on the counter.

Juliet was at a loss for what to say, hating that she'd crossed boundaries that only served to build a higher wall between them. "I'm sorry, my intent is not to upset you. I'll be out in a minute to help as soon as I rinsed the rest of these dishes and clean up."

"Fine." Jake headed out the door, pausing only long enough to look at the basket of flowers sitting on the coffee table. His expression darkened, the exact opposite of the effect she'd hoped to have on him.

After the work on the truck was finished, Juliet waited while Jake put away the last of the tools. In an odd way, the realization her time at the cabin had ended brought her no joy. Despite a few setbacks, Jake had been determined to get it fixed. Whether fueled by the hope she'd put in an application and soon help the town out of their dilemma, or whether in an effort to get rid of her—she wasn't sure.

They walk side-by-side as they headed back to the cabin. "I appreciate you taking the time to run me to town. Maybe it'll be a good chance for you to pick up extra food supplies, considering the three of us came by unexpectedly and used up a lot of your resources." Juliet laughed.

"I was thinking the same thing. So, what are your plans, besides putting in an application at the medical center? I realize my getting sick put a kink in your hiking plans."

"Well, I'm sure it'll take weeks before I hear anything back, so I was thinking about finding my way back to Memphis. Then if I need to come down for an interview, I can drive here. It'll be more convenient that way."

"I see. Or you could just stick around town and wait to hear from the clinic," Jake offered.

"I do have the vacation time, but I may need that to go back and forth during the interview and hiring process." Juliet drew up short, spotting a blur of red crossing the field off to the right.

"Look," she said, pointing toward the animal. "It's a fox. Do you think it's the same one?"

"It wouldn't surprise me. As a matter of fact, I think you're right. This one's still sporting a small limp on the same injured leg."

"Why is she stopping to watch us? Do you think she's come back to tell you thank you?" Juliet asked.

Jake shook his head. "That's a sweet thought, but then totally in character for you."

Another compliment—except it sounded like a backhanded one. "What's that supposed to mean?" She couldn't help but dig deeper, not because she wanted to hear him sing her praises, but because getting him to talk would help her learn more about Jake. If she was leaving, she was also out of time to help him. Unless she got the job. And if she did, it would be a clear sign she was supposed to be here and then she could help Jake. After all, he was the one who told her about the job in the first place.

"You figure it out. I'm going to grab my camera and get some pictures." He was gone before she could answer.

Jake returned and started to adjust the dials on the camera, and then started clicking away, taking picture after picture of the fox. "Will you add her to the pictures on the wall?

He paused, looking up at her as if wondering what to say.

"It's not like it isn't obvious you took the pictures hanging in the cabin. They are quite beautiful."

"It's not something I go around telling people. But yes, they're mine. And yes, if I can get a good shot, I'll hang it up."

"Do you think if I left you my email address, you could send me one? I'd love to have it printed and put on the wall. It's kind of a special moment. I've actually touched that fox, which makes it personal."

"Sentimental much?" He grinned. Jake returned to snapping a couple more photos before they stood silently together, watching the fox amble off across the meadow. "Come on, we should get going. I'll drop you at the clinic and you can make whatever arrangements you need to." Jake was clearly eager to be rid of her.

"Sounds good." She finished packing her stuff in her backpack, and it wasn't long before they were ready to head to town.

Jake headed down the bumpy road. Although, it was more like a path with worn down grass and ruts. He wound his way through the property. The tall trees, blanketed in green with hints of yellow as the temperatures started to change, a sign of fall just around the corner. An occasional bird crossing in front of them. The place was peaceful and nothing you'd find in the city.

He pointed out a few areas explaining the significance, but other than that, there wasn't much to say. Small talk wasn't Jake's forte. Twenty-five minutes later, they turned onto a paved road and not long after that, they crossed the state line and entered Tennessee. It wasn't long before she saw the sign: *Welcome to Hollow Creek.*

Juliet looked around, appreciating the sidewalk-lined streets and people hustling from store to store. Most of the buildings were painted wood with front porches to display their wares and signs. A few people waved at Jake as they meandered down the road, townsfolk recognizing him and his vehicle. Much to her surprise, Jake waved back. On second thought, she wasn't surprised. It was the other side of Jake she fully believed existed.

He pulled up in front of one of the larger buildings, the sign announcing they'd arrived at the Hollow Creek Medical Center. The building appeared to have been freshly painted, beautiful rosebushes lined the front walkway, and rocking chairs were lined up on the front porch to welcome everyone. Juliet couldn't think of a better or more original waiting area.

"Here you go," Jake said, reaching out to touch her arm as she pushed open the door. "Listen, I'm sorry if I wasn't always as nice as I could have been. I won't win any awards for being the perfect host, but I do want to tell you thank you for taking care of me."

Juliet covered his hand with hers. "You're welcome. It wasn't so bad. And it's a mutual thank you." She grinned. "Also, I appreciate the heads up about the job. Who knows, maybe we'll meet again someday soon."

"Maybe. I'll leave it up to you."

Juliet was confused by the comment, but Jake had already restarted the truck and she took her cue to leave. She grabbed her backpack out of the bed of the truck and waved, watching as he pulled away. Walking up the sidewalk to the medical center, she pushed open the door and walked in.

A young, redheaded woman greeted her with a sunshine happiness that was infectious. "Welcome to Hollow Creek Medical Center. I haven't seen you around here before. I'm sorry to have to tell you we don't have a doctor on staff now. If you need medical assistance, the best I can tell you is to head to Gatlinburg. It's about a forty-five-minute drive north of here."

Tough break for the residents in town and her information coincided with Jake's. "Actually, I'm here to see about a job. I'm a nurse with my APRN certification at a city hospital in Memphis. I heard you might have an opening and I'm interested. At least temporarily, until you find a doctor, that is."

The woman's eyes narrowed. "You heard?"

"Jake Kensington told me all about it. I ran into some trouble out on the Appalachian trail and he had to step in to help me. My friends and I stayed with him for a few days."

The woman's gaze sharpened. "Jake Kensington, huh? Did he say anything else?"

"No. I happened to mention I was looking for a change in my life and he suggested I apply here. He said he got an email about the opening from someone." Juliet shrugged, not sure where this conversation was headed.

"He did, did he? The woman was acting strange, but not in a bad way. Her smile was still firmly in place. "And you're a nurse?"

"Yes."

The woman's smile brightened even more, if it were possible. She jumped up from her chair. "My name is Olivia Livingston, and I'm the receptionist here. We have an online application system, and since you're only visiting the area, you can use my computer to fill it out."

"That sounds great." Juliet sat down in the chair Olivia indicated.

The receptionist reached over her shoulder to pull up the website and a few clicks later, the application was on the screen. "There you go."

"Thank you."

"My pleasure, trust me."

Juliet shot a quick look at the woman, unsure what she meant, but remained quiet as she tried to navigate the application.

"So, you say you've been staying in Jake's for the past few days?" Olivia asked.

"Yes, I got sick. Then, when my friends and I were ready to leave, Jake fell ill, and I stayed there to take care of him. Kind of one of those what goes around comes around, and this time, it was a virus that was going around," Juliet said, grinning up at the woman.

"Interesting." Olivia nodded, a little humming noise coming from her throat.

Juliet continued to fill out the form, trying to recall everything from memory. It's not like she walked around with a resume in purse. It might be better if she emailed one in when she got back home, just to cover the bases. "So, what happened to the doctor that was here? Jake mentioned he took a big city job in New York or something. If only he knew what he was heading into. Me, I personally like the slower pace and think this would be idyllic."

"*Hmphhh*," Olivia snorted. "I knew the guy was a short-termer when he got here, but we were desperate, so Dr. K hired him. He spent more time flying around the country for interviews than he did trying to get to know folks in town."

"Dr. K?"

"Dr. K owns the Medical Center," Olivia said, the expression on her face unreadable.

"Then why doesn't Dr. K work here? Is he older and retired now?" Juliet pressed for more information.

"Far from it. Such a sad story. Poor man lost his wife and has never really recovered. Quit practicing. Course the town keeps hoping he'll come back one day. Now would be nice, considering we just lost the other doctor."

The conversation about the doctor had taken a personal turn, but Juliet wanted to know what she was getting into. "But why would he stop practicing after his wife died? You would think most people would turn to their work as an escape from their pain, not the other way around."

"Well, I reckon it won't hurt to let you in on things just in case you get the job. Not that I'm a gossiper or anything. But Dr. K blames himself for his wife's death and feels that, as a medical professional, he should have been able to save her. He's wrong, you know. Dr. K's a nice guy, but he's not God." Olivia crossed the room and poured a cup of coffee, returning to her side. "Coffee?" she asked, holding it out to Juliet.

The caffeine this late would keep her wide awake into the night. "No, thanks. And that sounds awful. What a terrible burden to bear. I feel sorry for him."

"Most of us do that know the story, but you'll have none of it from me. Cause I'm not a gossiper, like I said. Just need-to-know stuff." Olivia took a sip of the coffee and leaned over Juliet's shoulder to see what she was typing.

"So, is that how the office stays open? He simply keeps his license hanging here and hires in medical professionals to fill the staff needs?"

"You catch on fast. Bonus points. I'll be sure to tell Dr. K," Olivia said, shooting her a wink. It was as if she was missing some important piece of information that Olivia didn't seem prone to sharing.

"Thanks. I'm a nurse, but do you think that would work? Just temporarily until your Dr. K finds a doctor, though."

"I reckon if you got hired, Dr. K will find a way to convince you to stay. Trust me on this."

"That may be true, but I've not decided it's a good permanent move for me yet. There," she said, typing her name on the signature line at the bottom. "I'm finished. All that's left is to hit send."

"Then do it." Olivia hovered close by, urging her to finish what she'd started.

"I just pray this is the right thing. I haven't even spoken to my boss about the possibility, but then I reckon I have weeks to cross that bridge. I'm a little nervous pressing send."

"Then here," Olivia said, leaning over and pressing the send button for her. "Done."

"Okay, then—I guess it is. I should get going. It was nice meeting and talking with you. Any idea how long it'll take before I hear back? What the timeframe is?"

"I know Dr. K's pretty anxious to find somebody soon because right now, the town has no one. I'm certain if the right person applied, they'd hear back sooner than later." The woman had an all-knowing gleam in her eyes, but then she probably understood how this office ran better than anyone.

"That sounds great. Thanks for all your help," Juliet said, walking toward the door.

"Same to you. I'm almost positive this will work out and I'll be seeing you again soon. I look forward to it."

"Thanks." Juliet stepped out onto the front porch and glanced around. She needed to make arrangements to get home, but she also needed to stop and breathe and take in the magnitude of the steps she had just taken, albeit with a little help from her new friend.

Juliet walked down the street, her stomach rumbling the alert that it was time to eat, even though by most people's standards, it was still early for dinner. She spotted a place called the Country Café and made her way inside. The sign on the front door indicated the early-bird specials and Juliet was always happy to take advantage of the special offers and the opportunity to save a few dollars.

The server called out a friendly greeting, and Juliet took a seat at the counter. After reviewing the menu, she decided what to order and pulled out her phone, hoping for a signal and a chance to check her messages for the first time in almost a week.

She played through all of them, but only three popped out as important. One, her mom called to check on her. Two, Jennifer was frantic to find out why she hadn't returned as scheduled. Her roommate and best friend always was something of a worrier. Something Juliet should have thought about before now. People would be worried.

The third call was the one she wanted to hear the most. Laura and Blaire had made it to the checkout point at Newfound Gap and were both safely back in Memphis. Of course, the *maybe we can laugh about this someday* comment made her laugh about the situation now.

Juliet ordered dinner and then sat back, using the opportunity to scope out the place. She replayed the conversation with the receptionist, her heart going out to the poor Dr. K. There was something about the whole thing that still bothered her, but she couldn't quite figure it out. Taking a sip of her tea, she paused, her cup stopping midair.

Dr. K.

Jake Kensington.

Was the K short for Kensington? He had a medical bag, and he definitely knew what he was doing. He'd also lost his wife, and it didn't appear he did much else besides helping the county sheriff on occasion. And take wildlife photos. A loner with a good cause. All the signs pointed in one direction. Dr. K had to be Jake.

How many people would match that description? But why wouldn't he just come right out and tell her the truth? Would she have still applied for the job? The thought of working for Jake made her heart beat faster. Work and relationships didn't work, not to mention, he didn't come close to her requirement that the man be a Christian.

It was too late to take back the application. And if Dr. K really was Jake, did that mean she had a far better chance at getting the job than she first suspected? After all, he was the one who pressed her to apply. And if Jake really was Dr. K, she'd stay, if only to help him.

The idea of sticking around town for a few days hit her and stuck. It would give her a chance to figure out if this was what she really wanted to do with her life. Temporarily, she reminded herself. But that meant she needed grounding, if she didn't intend to let her heart get involved or carried away. And who better to remind her than her dad? Some good old fatherly advice was in order.

And she needed to call Jennifer. Her roommate was used to Juliet's spur of the moment decisions, but even this one would shock her friend. The only downside was bailing on her share of the rent if she left. Her friend owned the house, and Juliet rented a room from her. The loss of income might be a problem, and she wouldn't want to do anything that put Jennifer in a bind. But then, temporary might be short enough it didn't matter, and Juliet could afford both places.

Chapter Nine

♥

JULIET MOVED TO ONE of the tables after letting the server know she was moving. With her water in one hand and her phone in the other, she slid into a booth. She checked the time, and dialed her father's number, hoping he wasn't busy with one of the parishioners.

"Hey, Daddy," Juliet said when he answered. "Just calling to check in."

"I'm so glad you did. Your mother was starting to worry when she didn't hear that you'd gotten home safely after the hike. Is everything all right, sweetheart?"

"I'm fine. You and mom can stop worrying—about that, anyway." She shook her head and laughed.

"What's that mean? Do you need me to come and get you? Wire you money? Are you in some sort of trouble with the law?" The urgency in his voice reflected his level of worry all too clearly. She was daddy's little girl and worrying about her was his job. At least, that's what he always told her when she was growing up.

"I'm fine, honestly. So relax. I got sick while we were on the hike and had to stay a few days with someone who helped me get through it. Which is in part what I wanted to talk to you about if you have a few minutes?"

"Sure thing, Pumpkin. For you, I make time. What's up?" he asked.

After filling him in with an expanded version of what happened and how it resulted in her taking care of Jake, she decided to plow into the crux of the call. "I applied for a job in Hollow Creek. They need someone at the medical clinic. They're in a desperate situation after the last doctor just walked out and there's no one here for the people in town to see if they need medical care. Not until they hire someone, anyway."

"But why you? You have a job?" Juliet knew it was the first thing he'd ask, and it was the easier part to answer. The rest got a little more complicated.

"I know. I've been restless lately and thinking of shaking things up a bit. As a nurse, there's no job shortage, and this opportunity would be a chance for a new adventure."

"But that's over five hours away. You've never lived far away, and your mother would hate not having you around." She would be disappointed, but it was her dad that would hate it the most. Not being able to watch her every move. It's not that he didn't trust her; he did. It's just that he liked to watch over his daughter, much the way God wanted to watch over his people.

God trusted her to make the right decisions, and she needed the same trust from her dad. "It's only temporary, and you can visit me anytime. You love the mountains."

"What else is going on? This still isn't like you. I mean, are you serious about it?"

Her father knew her well, but it was time they both realized she wanted to experience more of life than she had so far. Try new things. "I haven't gotten the job yet, but yes, I'm serious. At first it might have been considered a bit of a rash decision, but then the more I thought about it, the more it sounded right."

"What else is going on?" he pressed.

She needed to tell him the truth. He wouldn't like it, but she'd tell him anyway. "It has a lot to do with the man I nursed back to health."

"What about *him*?" her father asked, his voice dropping a notch.

"Relax. Nothing happened. You know me. His wife died three years ago, and he's still in a lot of pain. I want to help him if I can. You taught me to help people when they are down and lost. And Jake is certainly lost. I have a sense God led me here to help him." It was a valid point, and she was glad she thought of it, knowing it would go a long way to smooth things over with him.

"But you don't quit a job and move away from your family and friends."

"Why not?" She shrugged, even though he couldn't see her.

"Because...I don't know. Because you're my daughter and I like you close to home."

And just like that, she'd won the discussion. He had nothing solid with which to stop her from making the decision. "I love you too, Daddy." Juliet grinned.

"And since Jake isn't the only reason I'm considering the move, it shouldn't be a problem. Helping the people in this town through a difficult transition would make me feel useful, not to mention give me a chance to check out other options in the medical field. Jake is just a side project." And that's all he could ever be. God may be calling her to help him, but he certainly wasn't pushing them together for anything else. The Bible and her parents were proof of that. The unequally yoked hadn't changed and wouldn't change by the time she left town.

"Juliet, what do I tell your mother?" he asked, grasping at straws.

"First of all, I haven't gotten the job yet. I applied. There's no guarantee I'll get it. I just wanted to let you know I'm considering it and that I'm okay. Jake's a nice guy, Daddy. Don't worry."

"*Hmmphhh*. A father's prerogative."

"I'm sure. Jake's clearly still in love with his late wife. Not to mention, he's not a Christian. And you know how I feel about that." Juliet asked her father once about the equally yoked aspect of marriage and the biblical implications. He hadn't exactly agreed with her, but he also told her that her walk with Jesus was her own unique journey and that she'd figure out the truth of hers as she got older. *Whatever that meant.*

"Okay, then. Keep me posted. When will you know and when are you coming home? I need something to appease your mother, who keeps hoping you'll move back to Dylan. Hollow Creek isn't exactly what she had in mind."

"I expect it will take weeks. I'm taking a few extra vacation days to check out the area, and then I'll be home."

"Sounds like a plan. Be safe and make good choices."

"I always do." *Or try to.*

"I know, Pumpkin, I know. Call me when you find out more."

Juliet hung up the phone, glad to have that out of the way. Next stop, Jennifer.

Her roommate answered on the first ring. "I'm so glad to hear from you. Is everything okay?" Jennifer asked.

"It is. Have you got a minute? I need to talk to you about something."

"Sure. I was just about to pick out a Hallmark movie for tonight."

"Ahh, yes. Hallmark movie night with the ladies. Tell everyone I said hello." That was only one of the things she would miss. Giving up her social outlets, including her small group at the church, and being further away from her family were all factors she hadn't considered. Maybe this wasn't such a good idea.

"Will do. What's up?" Jennifer asked.

Juliet proceeded to tell her roommate everything. Even more than she'd told her own father.

"Wow. That's a lot to take in. Do you have feelings for this Jake guy?" Jennifer asked.

"No, it's not like that." *Maybe a little*. But none that mattered. "I really think Jake is the doctor looking to hiring someone, but he's not exactly Mr. Let's Get Personal."

"I think it's a wonderful opportunity to do something different. You keep talking about mixing things up. Now's your chance. I say go for it." Jennifer was always good for an adventure and that's exactly how she was picturing this. But she was forgetting some of the down-to-earth aspects.

"What about my rent? If this turns out to be longer than just a few weeks, what will you do? The last thing I'd want is to leave you in the lurch with a mortgage payment that's hard to pay." Juliet was the more practical of the two.

"No worries. Lily asked me just the other day if I was willing to take in a third person. Which I wasn't, but she can have your room. If you get the job, that is. I'm not shoving you out the door," Jennifer said, laughing.

"You are so not like my father. He didn't take this well at all."

"Of course he didn't. What father wants his little girl to move to a place because of a man she just met? But it's your life. Be brave. Face these new challenges if you get a chance."

Juliet took a deep breath. "It's not because of Jake. Well, I mean, it is, sort of. But not in the way you mean. Oh, I don't know." She closed her eyes and tried to think.

"Juliet, you know exactly what you need to do."

"What's that?" she asked.

"I'm sure Hollow Creek has a church. Go visit it. Meet some people. See if you're comfortable. Pray about it. Search in your heart if it feels right. If not, rescind the application and come back to Memphis. If it does, stay there and do exactly what you planned. Check the place out." Since when did Jennifer become practical? Maybe years of living with her were rubbing off on her friend.

Juliet smiled. "Perfect advice and just what I needed to hear. Thank you so much."

"Anytime roomie, anytime. Keep me posted. On the job and Grizzly Jake. Got to run. Hugs."

Her friend hung up before Juliet could answer, and just as the food was delivered. By the time dinner was over, she'd decided to take her friend's advice.

Where better to find answers than at church?

Chapter Ten

♥

JULIET STEPPED OUT INTO the waning sunshine, letting it warm her face. "Excuse me, ma'am." She took a step toward the woman walking down the sidewalk.

The older woman stopped and smiled at her. "What is it, dearie?"

"I was wondering if you could tell me where the church is?"

The woman's smile broadened, if it were possible. "Such a lovely place, it is. Pastor James and his wife have been around for a long time. He should still be there now; if you hurry, you can catch up with him."

"I don't know if I need to go that far." Juliet laughed. Actually, she wanted to go further. She wanted to talk to the highest authority in search of peace regarding her choices.

"It's just down the street about four blocks; turn left and go about a block, and you'll see it on your right. It's the Faith Christian church. If you're looking for a particular denominational church, there are some others over in Willow, the next town north of here."

"No, the Faith Christian sounds perfect. Thank you for your help."

"Any time. I'd walk with you there if I didn't have to stop and see my son first."

"That's sweet of you. Have a nice visit with your son," Juliet said. So far, the people she met in town were rather nice. Quite the contradiction to the original grizzly Jake she'd met, but way more like the teddy bear Jake she suspected him to be.

Juliet followed the woman's directions and found the church quite easily. It was a small, white building with a high-pointed steeple. Very traditional. The oversized brown double doors at the front made her smile. They look just like the one's back home where her father preached. Quaint came to mind. As she reached to open the door, Juliet realized it was almost as though she were being welcomed home. She held the door lightly as it closed, respectful of the sanctuary silence.

She looked around, admiring the beautiful stained-glass windows that surrounded the room, casting it in a beautiful glow. Juliet moved toward the front, loving the large cross at the back of the stage area. Judging by the placement of the chairs and the organ, they were still very much a community that embraced traditional church music, something her father had changed in his own house of worship. Juliet liked the new upbeat music that many of the churches were embracing, the praise and worship teams lifting people's voices together in song and praising God in an upbeat manner. There was something to be said for both ways since considering the traditional music was more reverent and peaceful.

Juliet moved to sit in the front row and bowed her head.

Father God, I pray that you will guide me and show me the way regarding this big decision in my life. I know I've grown impatient wanting the love of a Christian man with which to share the joys of love and family. I realize that might not be Your plan for me. Maybe my plan is to be of help to others. Whatever it is, Lord, I trust you. In Jesus' name I pray for you to show me the way, Lord. Amen

Juliet sat back on the pew and took a deep breath. The serenity of the sanctuary filled her, and she let out a deep cleansing breath. She thought back to the many times over the years that she'd sat in the front row. It had been expected of her as the pastor's daughter, not to mention a way for her parents to keep a close eye on her. They'd kept a tight rein, wanting her to always make good choices. And all through her childhood they'd been there to help her with those decisions. But then came adulthood and the ability to make her own decisions, and she could only hope she'd make the right one now.

She got up and started to leave, stopping for one last look around the place before she left. The peace in her heart was calming, the fears and doubts she'd had walking in now gone. In its place was the knowledge that although she didn't know the answer yet, she was confident it would come to her by the time she was faced with the decision.

Juliet made her way back to Main Street and to the motel she'd noticed when they'd first entered Hollow Creek. Without a vehicle at her disposal, she could only hope they had a room and that their vacancy sign was accurate. Catching a ride back to Jake's wasn't what she had in mind, and the odds of a bus passing through to take her to the next town were slim to none.

It didn't take her long to reach the Sleepy Hollow motel. Juliet smiled at the name, remembering the movie she once watched that had left her sleepless for days. It was an ironic name for a motel, a good indicator that the owner had a weird sense of humor.

She pushed open the door, a buzzer sounding in the back room to signal her arrival.

A portly man came out from the office. "How can I help you?" he asked.

"I noticed your vacancy sign, and I'd like a room for two nights, please. It might be more, but at this point two will do."

"Is it just you?" he asked, one eyebrow raised.

"Yes. I'm considering moving into town and wanted to check the area out."

The man looked her over and nodded. "I see. In that case, I'll give you our local discount rate. The locals around here send a lot of business my way when their families come into town and they don't have enough space." He smiled and grabbed the key out of the drawer.

"I just need your driver's license and a credit card. The discounted rate is fifty a night, and I'll put a hold on your card until you check out for the hundred dollars plus tax. If you decide to stay longer, I'll just adjust it. Is that okay?" he asked, typing in some information on the computer.

His offer was quite welcome as it would go much easier on her budget and allow her to indulge in a few things while she was here—like meals out. "That sounds perfect. And thank you. That's kind of you."

"The town likes it when young folk consider moving here. We lose too many to the big city, so it's nice to see it in reverse."

"I'm from the city, and trust me, I much prefer the quietness of Hollow Creek."

He handed her the key. "I've put you in the room at the end. Go out the front door and turn left. It'll be the last door on the end. That's one of the units with a kitchenette, just in case you don't want to eat all your meals out or if you're on a budget."

"Thank you. That's very considerate of you." Juliet took the key, slid her backpack over her shoulder again, and headed out the door, waving at the man. Chalk another positive point up to Hollow Creek residents.

Juliet entered the room and was pleasantly surprised at how clean and upbeat the room had been decorated. Nothing like she expected based on the name of the place. She put her backpack on the bed and sat down at the table in front of the window that looked outside the front of the hotel. She pulled out her phone, intent on sending Jennifer a message to let her know where she was staying and her game plan.

Her email icon was flashing, Juliet clicking on that first. She was surprised to see an email from the Hollow Creek Medical Center. Juliet frowned. A response that quick could only mean one thing—she'd been rejected.

Obviously, Dr. K *wasn't* Jake. Perhaps wishful thinking on her part.

Internet service wasn't the quickest. She watched as the blue circle spun around, trying to load. The email finally popped up on the screen.

Dear Juliet,

Dr. K asked me to forward his response to you.

Olivia

Dear Juliet Walker,

After reading your resume and reviewing your considerable experience, we would like to offer you the position of Advanced Practiced Registered Nurse at the Hollow Creek Medical Center, beginning immediately. As you know, our office is currently unstaffed and in dire need of a medical professional for the people in the town who need medical assistance. I will continue to look for a doctor, and I understand your need for this to be a temporary arrangement. Based on your qualifications, however, I would like to retain your services permanently if you change your mind, as the needs of the community have increased over the years and I see this as a benefit.

The terms of the employment offer are attached to this email. Please respond as soon as possible with your decision or any other questions you may have.

Dr. K

Hollow Creek Medical Center

Juliet - I realize this is a little unorthodox, but then, so is Dr. K. I felt certain you would get the job and, on a more personal note, hope you will accept. It would be lovely to work with you. Let me know your answer and I will forward it to Dr. K. I'm like the monkey in the middle. LOL.

Olivia

Juliet was shocked. The rejection she was sure she would receive was, in fact, an employment offer. Things didn't happen this fast in the real world. But then, Hollow Creek was like stepping back in time with its sidewalks, antiquated shops, and abundance of friendly people. The expediency was explained by the doctor, and Juliet understood the reasoning. She was also more certain now that the doctor was Jake.

As she prepared to write her answer and wondered what to say, she was surprised at the level of calmness she felt. She was going to say yes. She knew in her heart it was the right thing to do. Before she accepted anything, she needed to call her boss. Sandy had always been good to her and she wouldn't want to leave her in a lurch. Juliet dialed her number. "Hey, Sandy. I'm so glad you answered."

"Juliet? What a surprise. How are you? And how was your hike?"

"Well, about that. It turned out quite different than I planned." Talk about an understatement. "I ended getting sick and didn't get to complete the hike."

"What do you mean?"

"Long story short—I ended up with a virus that I must've picked up at the hospital. I stayed with a guy who came to my rescue. But then he got sick, and I stayed to nurse him back to health. The others finished the hike but I'm still in Hollow Creek."

"Him?" Sandy asked.

"Is that all you got from what I just told you?" Juliet laughed.

"Not all, but that was the most interesting piece." Sandy's directness was one of the things Juliet admired about the woman. You always knew where you stood with her.

"His name is Jake Kensington. He is something of a hermit around here. But honestly, he's a nice guy, so don't worry. But there's been this really strange twist of fate I need to talk to you about."

"I'm listening. Sounds interesting, especially if it involves a man."

"It's nothing like that. Trust me. It's just that Hollow Creek is a small community, and they lost their doctor to a city hospital recently. I found out they were looking for someone and was encouraged to apply. My thought was to make it temporary, just until they found a doctor to staff the medical center. I honestly thought I'd come home in a few days, talk it over with you, and wait it out to see what happened. Except, somehow, I was accepted and offered employment with them literally hours later."

"That's insane. With all the background checks and everything else that need to be run, who would do that?" It was the same thing Juliet had thought of.

"I have my suspicions, but they haven't been confirmed yet. I'll let you know when I know, but this is a lovely town and the people are friendly and it sort of fits. Me."

"Sounds like you want to accept. But then you wouldn't have put in an application if you weren't interested." Her boss knew her well. Most people did though, since she was like an open book.

"True, on both counts. I just don't want to make life tough on you with scheduling. They want me to start immediately. With no doctor in the office, the closest place they can get medical treatment is almost fifty miles away. You and I both know what that means."

"Listen, if your heart is telling you to accept this, and those people need you by the sound of it, then I say go for it. We have plenty of people here at the hospital that are willing to fill your shoes—but it sounds like they have no one. I'm sure I can rearrange the schedule. Take whatever time you need. Your job will be here waiting for you whenever you're ready to return."

Adrenaline coursed through Juliet as everything sunk in. She was going to do this. "I was hoping you'd say that, but I wanted to talk to you before I accepted."

"I'll clear it with Human Resources. Don't worry. I'm curious about how they're operating without a doctor. Have you checked into that to make sure everything is legitimate?"

"I have. Apparently, a doctor owns the place and keeps up his licensing requirements, but he no longer practices medicine. They had another doctor here for a couple of years, but then, like I said, he split for a big city offer." Juliet liked that her boss was concerned. As far as bosses went, she was the best. At least in Hollow Creek, her boss was a piece of paper hanging on a wall. Or he would be until Juliet met him. There was no way she would take the job without finding out more about the man. Or Jake, if what she suspected was true.

"Why doesn't the other guy practice anymore? Is he retired or what's his story?"

"I get the feeling from what I'm hearing that he's been through a difficult time and hasn't recovered." She didn't want to discuss Jake's personal affairs. It somehow felt as though she would be crossing an imaginary line of their friendship.

"Interesting. It sounds like a great opportunity and a good chance for a change of pace. Maybe this is exactly what you needed."

"Thanks for the vote of confidence and the approval. It means a lot to me."

The two women talked a few more minutes before Juliet hung up, more confident than ever in her decision. *She would stay, but only on one condition.*

Dear Olivia

Thank you for your kind words. I too feel it would be a wonderful experience and a joy to work with you. Even if it is temporary. The full-time offer is generous, but not one I can accept at this point.

Please inform Dr. K of my conditional acceptance of his employment offer. Conditional because although I agree to all the terms and look forward to joining you at the Hollow Creek Medical Center, I'm not comfortable accepting employment from someone I've never met. Please communicate to Dr. K that in order to finalize the paperwork, I would expect to meet with him in person.

Juliet

If the doctor was willing to jump this fast into hiring her, Juliet was certain he wouldn't let one small meeting interfere with those plans. She sent a note to Jennifer letting her know of the crazy new twist in her life. It looked like she wouldn't be staying here for a few days. Instead, it looked like she was moving here. At least temporarily.

She held off sending a message to her parents, realizing that it would be better to give them a few days to get used to the *idea* of her moving to a new location before she bombarded them with the reality.

Chapter Eleven

♥

THE OVERHEAD DOORBELL BUZZED as Juliet pushed the front door open at the medical clinic. Even knowing with an almost positive certainty that Jake would turn out to be Dr. K, it was a shock to come face-to-face with the real Dr. K...or Dr. Kensington, as was the case. A man who looked every inch the professional.

So much so that it had taken her longer to assimilate the two men as one in the same, and zero in on the similarities versus focusing on the differences. His clean-shaven face and shortcut hair revealed an attractive man underneath all the scruffy hair he recently sported. The eyes were the same—warm and kind, but everything else was different. Her heart raced in a way it hadn't in a long time, as though recognizing someone special. The combination of knowing him by his eyes and yet admiring him from the outside had collided and burst into what could only be called attraction.

Jake stepped forward to greet her and extended his hand. "Dr. K," he said unabashedly. "It's nice to see you again, and I'm very happy you accepted the position."

That's it? Who was he kidding? "Umm...hello to you to...So why the subterfuge?"

"I just didn't see telling you as necessary. I like to keep my private life private. Fewer questions that way. And I figured I had a better shot at you accepting the position given our history."

"Our history? I'm lost."

"Okay, so my history. As a grizzly bear." Jake smiled, and it was as if the sun had been shining in the office.

"So, Dr. K is actually Dr. Kensington?" she asked, making one hundred percent sure.

"One and the same. But I don't use either title if I don't have to anymore. I don't practice medicine, and that's the way I intend to keep it."

It was one thing to think it was possible and another to have it confirmed. He didn't even look much like Grizzly Jake, except for his eyes. They were the same. "So why the sudden change in appearance?"

Jake shrugged. "I didn't want to scare you off. I thought maybe you should see a professional employer who is asking you to stay and join the team."

"Team?"

"Olivia and the new doctor, once I find one. I've sent a notice to the Sunshine Employment Agency and hope they can find someone soon who would be willing to practice in a small community."

"I never agreed to stay on. I have a job in Memphis. Officially, I'm only here until you find a new doctor. I can't get over the change in your appearance. If it weren't for your eyes, I might not have believed it myself. You look good."

"I'm glad you approve. Now that you've met me, do you unconditionally accept the position?"

"Of course." Juliet's expression softened as she realized what all the pieces meant as they fell into place. "Why don't you show me around the office and let me know what you expect?"

"That sounds great," Jake said, pulling open the door leading to the back offices and holding it open for Juliet, as he indicated for her to pass through. The man had even splashed on a woodsy-scented cologne that made her take a little deeper breath to savor the scent.

Juliet tried to focus on the professional aspects of the meeting, otherwise her brain would turn to mush. Jake Kensington was incredibly handsome beneath the gruff exterior. The problem was she'd liked him before the change. After the change was where the real problem started. She couldn't help but think of him as a man and not her boss.

Accepting the job had never depended on whether Jake and Dr. K were one and the same; she'd known in her heart this was the right thing to do. The next step for her. Forcing Jake out of his shell was now the next step for her and for Jake, but he just didn't know it yet. Her silly heart needed to understand Jake was off-limits in every way other than as a professional relationship.

He'd gone to great pains to clean up—for her. Maybe that's why her heart and brain were having trouble understanding and accepting the way things had to remain between them. After all, Jake had known it would be her. Was the doctor trying to win over the nurse to work in his clinic like he said, or was it more than that?

Juliet tried to focus on what he was saying as he pointed out the different rooms and the specialized equipment he'd installed. "I like the way you've laid everything out—quite sensible. And I'm sure your patients appreciate the relaxing decor. I'm glad you didn't go with the starchy whites like a lot of places tend to do."

"When I designed it, calm and peaceful was what I had in mind. I appreciate that you noticed."

"I know I promised not to cross into personal lines back at the cabin, but I find this is different. Working together as professionals, I feel I deserve to know the answer to a few things." Getting to know Jake was the only way she could help him, and she had to start somewhere.

She sensed his hesitation even before he answered. "I'll answer only if I think you need to know. How's that?"

"It'll do. Why are you looking for a doctor?" She knew what the receptionist had told her, but she wanted to hear it from Jake, hoping it would open a line of communication between them.

"I would've thought that was obvious. The office needs one. No offense, but there's only so much you're allowed to do as a nurse who's APRN certified—legally."

She wasn't letting him off that easily. "I understand that. But the town already has a doctor. *You.*"

Jake turned to face the window, shutting her out. "That's a closed chapter of my life."

She took a few steps closer. "Maybe it's a chapter you need to reopen. You took an oath. How can you walk away from the talents that you've been given? God-given talents. You're letting them go to waste and it doesn't seem right from where I'm sitting. Help me to understand." If she was going to help him, it was important to push him out of his comfort zone.

He turned back to face her; his mouth set in a firm line. Waves of tension radiated toward her. "It's none of your business. Why I don't practice, that is. And it's not like I didn't see the look in your eyes earlier. I know Olivia's told you at least some of the story. So, let's not sugarcoat this. I already told you my wife died. What you may not know is that the people in town all know I was responsible. At what point do you think I would still have the town's confidence in my abilities? And more importantly, the confidence in my own abilities?"

What was he talking about? It's not exactly what Olivia had told her. "Jake, it's not that way. Tell me about it. Tell me what happened. Help me to understand."

"It's personal—and none of your business. I think we should stick to keeping things on a professional level. I have a lot to show you, and a lot to go over. Perhaps we should focus on that." Jake had drawn a line in the sand and dug in his feet, unwilling to be pulled to the other side. Juliet had no choice but to accept his decision, at least for now. God never promised the road to helping someone would be easy, and Juliet was determined to do something right.

"Fine. Then take me to lunch and tell me everything you think I need to know." She wasn't done with him yet, but moving into town would give her plenty of time to offer her support. He didn't want her sympathy and she would do well to remember that in the future. Besides, Jake would have plenty of women in Hollow Creek ready to offer their own version of help, especially if he kept this new clean look. Somehow, the thought of other women vying for his attention didn't set well with her. She'd have to think about that later, but right now, she needed to focus on learning everything she could about the medical center and her responsibilities.

"Sounds good. The diner's just down the street. It will give us a chance to relax and discuss everything that needs discussing." Jake led the way back out of the office, stopping only at the front desk.

"Juliet has accepted and will start work in the morning. I've given her the keys already, and she'll be here at eight. We're going over to the diner to discuss some of the smaller details if you need me for anything."

"Welcome aboard, Juliet. Have a nice lunch you two," Olivia said, shooting Juliet a wink when Jake wasn't looking. The receptionist had it all wrong.

This was business, not a date.

Chapter Twelve

♥

JULIET HAD BEEN WORKING at the clinic for over a week and there was still no word from Jake. Dr. Kensington, that is. It hadn't taken her any time at all to fall in with the setup of the office; the clinic was designed with ultramodern equipment considering it was small-town USA. And Olivia was a goldmine of information when it came to the patients. She was like a walking encyclopedia of the people in town, cutting out much of the time Juliet would normally spend reading entire files to catch up on medical history. Instead, she was able to stick to the key facts.

It was an unusually slow day and the perfect opportunity to take an early lunch. Flexibility was another perk of working in a small-town office she hadn't known about. "Olivia, I'm going to head out to run a couple of errands and get some lunch. Call me if anything comes up."

The receptionist grinned. "You'll be fine. Today is the 15th and a Friday. It's a payday and everyone else will be out doing the same thing you are—running errands and paying bills." Olivia laughed.

"Works for me. Want me to bring you back anything?" They both enjoyed the deli sandwiches from Platters Sandwich Shop and had started taking turns buying each other lunch.

"Of course." Olivia pulled out the menu she kept nearby, perusing her choices. "Pimento cheese on a baguette," she said, tapping the item on the menu. "And French fries and a sweet tea to drink." It still surprised Juliet that Hollow Creek had a deli fancy enough to serve something so fashionably on point in the city delis. One more thing that made her feel right at home.

"Sounds great. I might have to do the same. See you in about an hour."

"Will do." Olivia went back to working on her computer and Juliet headed out the door, into the sunshine.

She strolled to the bank first, determined to open up an account and get her current bank balances transferred locally. It might not be permanent, but it would make her life easier. "Good morning, Mrs. Dooley." Juliet smiled at the kindly woman whom she'd met a couple of days ago at the clinic.

"Good heavens, Dr. Walker, call me Linda. No need for formalities around here."

"Well, in that case, call me Juliet. Especially since I'm a nurse, not a doctor." She laughed. "I'd like to open an account."

"Of course, dearie. Here, just grab a seat and fill out this paperwork, and I'll get Traci Lawton, our bank manager, to fix you right up."

"And here I thought I was the one who had to do the fixing up," Juliet teased.

"True enough, but let's hope it's not me that needs the fixing." The older woman grinned and handed her the paperwork.

Juliet made her way to the seating area, choosing the armchair as it looked the most comfortable. She reached in her purse for a pen just as her phone rang. Olivia's name popped up on the screen, causing her a bit of worry. Hopefully, the receptionist was only looking to change her order.

"Juliet," she answered, holding her breath as she waited.

"It's me, Olivia. Come quick. Little Johnny Trenton's got a fishhook embedded in his arm. It looks really bad. His mother has it wrapped, but the bleeding hasn't stopped."

Juliet didn't need to hear anymore. "I'm on my way." She shoved the account application in her purse and raced out the door, rushing down the street to the clinic. Swiping her scan card to enter the back area, she ran to the room where she could hear Olivia trying to calm the boy. Inside, she spotted the child cradling his arm, a bloody bandage wrapped around it. His face was ashen and tear-streaked, and she jumped into action to take over the situation.

"I'm Juliet Walker and I'm a nurse here. I'm going to help you, okay?" she said, trying to comfort the child.

He nodded, but her words didn't take away the fear in his eyes.

"Will he be all right?" the mother asked, standing close by her son, one hand on his shoulder, as if to reassure him.

"Let me look and assess the wound, but I'm sure he'll be fine. How old are you, Johnny?" she asked, trying to draw the kid into conversation. Anything to take his mind off the injury.

"Twelve," he said, his face tight with pain.

"Olivia, can you get me the Fentanyl and Versed. Let's see what we can do to ease his pain and make him more comfortable."

Juliet turned back to Johnny. "Why don't you tell me what you were doing when this happened."

"Fishing." He sniffed.

"I know that. But where? And what were you fishing for?" Juliet grabbed several sterile bandages, laying them close by. She started to unwrap his arm, conscious that every move could cause more pain, or worse, push the hook in further.

"I was down at the lake fishing for bass," Johnny answered, his lower lip trembling as he used his good arm to brush at his face.

"Have any luck?" She had to keep him talking.

"I did." Johnny shot her a half grin, half grimace. "I caught three before I got stupid and did this." Apparently, talking about what you caught was a universal joy for people of all ages.

"It sounds like you're very experienced at fishing. We call these accidents, young man, not stupidity." The bleeding had slowed, and Juliet carefully checked the wound. It was a treble hook and two of the barbs had lodged deeply into his muscle. The only way to get it out was surgically, something she wasn't authorized to do. And exactly why they needed a doctor in residence.

"It really hurts." He grimaced.

"I know and I'm sorry." Olivia returned with the meds she'd requested, and Juliet proceeded to measure out the proper dose for Johnny's age and weight. He was going to need it, considering she needed time to figure out the next step. They had a doctor in charge, and if Juliet had anything to say about it, the man was going to do his job—whether he liked it or not.

Dr. K had been hiding out in the mountains long enough.

After giving him the shot to ease his pain and help him relax, Juliet re-wrapped Johnny's arm in a clean bandage. "Olivia, if you can hold his arm, putting a little pressure near the hook but not on it, that would be great. I'll be right back."

Olivia looked at her, the question in her eyes clear. Luckily, she was smart enough not to ask in front of the patients.

"It's bad, isn't it?" Johnny asked, fear in his voice.

"It is, but nothing we can't manage," Juliet answered, praying she was right. She left the room quickly to avoid more questions and made her way to her office.

She dialed Jake's number, hoping he'd answer.

"Hello," he said, his deep husky voice helping to restore her calm.

"Hey, it's Juliet. We need you at the clinic. *I* need you to come to the clinic. *Stat.*"

"You know I don't work there—and you know why. I trust your medical opinion, but if it's over your level, send the patient to the ER in Gatlinburg."

"That's almost an hour away. Come on, Jake. It's Johnny Trenton. He's a twelve-year-old boy with a treble hook buried deep in the muscle. I can't do the surgical procedure or the stitches and we both know it. But you can. You're the doctor in charge at the clinic since you haven't found anyone to take Dr. Brown's place—whether you like it or not."

"Johnny Trenton?" Jake repeated the name as if hoping he'd heard her wrong.

"Yes. Do you know him?"

"Know him? I helped deliver him." Jake let out a deep sigh, not even bothering to hide it from her. "This won't work. What if I can't help him? Or worse, it goes horribly wrong?" Jake asked, the fear in his voice radiating loud and clear.

"Please," she begged. "Help me. Remember, you took an oath. Just like I did. *We* have to help him."
Her plea was met with silence. *Please, Lord, give him the courage to do this.*

"Fine. I'll be there in twenty minutes if I step on it."

"Thank you," she said softly, letting out the deep breath she'd been holding.

"Thank me if nothing goes wrong," he muttered as he hung up the phone.

Juliet kept a watch out for Jake and was relieved when, twenty minutes later, he showed up dressed in a white clinical jacket. This was a newer version of Jake that she'd yet to meet. Dr. Kensington in take charge mode and ready for action. Apparently, twenty minutes was all it took to get him mentally prepared.

"Glad you're here, Dr. K." Juliet shot him a quick smile. "You'll be fine...so relax. They're in room two, waiting. The treble hook has two barbs lodged deep in the muscle. I've cleaned the wound and re-wrapped it to help stop the bleeding, trying to stabilize him until you arrived. X-rays are negative for bone damage and they are in the room if you want to take a look."

"Thanks. Sounds like you have it all under control." They walked in the room, poor Johnny's color as ashen as when she left. He had every right to be afraid, not to mention the fishhook lodged in his arm had to be extremely painful.

"Thank goodness you're here, Dr. K," Mrs. Trenton said, worry lines creasing her face. "Juliet explained what's going on and that you were on your way. That's when I knew this would all be okay. You're the best."

"I'll do my best, Mary." He turned to Juliet. "Did you give him pain reliever?" Jake asked, falling right back into a medical care routine that came from experience.

"I did. Twenty-five mcg of Fentanyl and 5 mg of Versed to help him relax. They're already starting to work and he's managing his pain level much better."

"Perfect. Tetanus shot?"

"Not yet. Thought you should look at the wound and the hook first. He had one four years ago. We could just do a booster, but we'll let you decide."

Jake unwound the bandage. "Hey, Johnny. Sorry about this, buddy. We'll get you fixed up in no time."

Juliet liked the confidence he portrayed to the child and his mother, even if he doubted his own abilities.

"Okay, Dr. K," Johnny said, rubbing away the tears on his cheeks, trying to be brave.

Jake could use a lesson out of the kid's playbook. He looked closely at the wound with the embedded hook, using a magnifying glass to get a closer look. "It's in there good, but nothing we can't manage. I need you to lie down," he said, putting his arm behind the boy to ease him back onto the pillows. "We're going to use a local anesthetic around the wound so you won't feel anything, but I'm going to surgically remove the barbs from the muscle and then we'll stitch you up. You'll be back fishing in no time at all," Jake said, shooting the boy a smile.

Juliet's heart melted at the sight. He really was good with patients.

"Okay, Dr. K. Not sure about the fishing part though. I may be done with that."

"Let's go with the tetanus booster, Juliet. It looks fairly clean, so good call. Also, can you set up a combo of lidocaine and epinephrine for the local?" He turned back to the boy. "And as for you, young man, there's no sense turning away from what you love. It's just an accident. I'll be expecting you to catch me a big catfish for my supper as repayment for services today."

Juliet wasn't sure Jake fully understood the advice he was giving the child. It was advice Jake himself would benefit from applying to his own life. The trouble, however, was finding the right way to help him see the truth. "Sure thing. I'll be right back with the local. Here's the booster," she said, handing him the syringe. Juliet shot him a smile...a small reward for his efforts so far, hoping to encourage him.

A few minutes later, Juliet returned and handed him the vial with the local anesthetic. "I've already set up the surgical tray and the stitch prep, so as soon as he's numb, we're ready."

Jake nodded. "This will pinch a bit, but nothing terrible. I promise."

Johnny nodded, although his color had gone a little paler.

Making quick work of the local, Jake was finished in short order. "Let's give this a minute or two to set in."

Jake checked over the instrument tray and pulled it close. He picked up Johnny's arm and tapped on a few test areas. "Can you feel my touch, Johnny?"

"Nope. Arm feels better too."

"That's partly the pain reliever and partly the local. You're being very brave, you know."

"Thanks," Johnny mumbled.

Jake went to work, using the scalpel to cut around the barbed areas with precision and care to get as little tissue as possible. She knew from experience this would help expedite the healing.

Together they worked as a team. She knew instinctively which instruments he needed—and when, earning several looks of surprise and an appraising glance for her efforts. Juliet also knew she could have managed the surgery, but two things kept her from resorting to such extremes. One, she wasn't licensed to do the procedure, even though by some standards it was considered minor. Two, it was a gifted opportunity to get Jake back in the office, one she wouldn't let go of lightly. Call it divine intervention if you will, but it worked.

Within fifteen minutes, the hook was out, and Jake had the boy stitched up. "You want this as a souvenir?" Jake asked, holding the hook up for Johnny to see.

"*Umm*, sure."

His mother reached to take it. "Doesn't do much for me, but boys are different, I reckon." She let out a deep breath. "I can't thank you enough for coming in to help, Dr. K. Juliet's a lovely nurse and was amazing the way she managed things until you got here. You two make a wonderful team. You've been missed. It just wasn't the same with the other Doc. He didn't seem to love and connect with the community the way you once did. Hollow Creek needs you back."

Juliet looked over at Jake and grinned. "Dr. K gets all the credit here. I'm only the assistant. And I agree...Hollow Creek does need him back."

Jake flushed red. "Thanks. Glad I could help." He left the room without another word.

Juliet finished up, giving instructions to Johnny and his mother. "I'll be back after I get your paperwork printed to send home with you. He'll need to get an appointment with an orthopedic doctor as a follow up to make sure there's no muscle damage." She headed down the hall in search of Jake and found him in the office. He stood staring out the window, as though lost in thought, not noticing she'd come into the room.

"Great job, Dr. K.," Juliet said, getting his attention.

He turned to face her, the joy on his face undeniable. Jake crossed the room to her side and took her hands. "We did it. I can't thank you enough for calling me and leaving me with no other choice but to show up. Best thing you could have done."

Jake hugged Juliet, surprising her even more, if it were possible. The new Jake would be hard to resist like this, non-believer or otherwise. Forget that her heart skipped a beat in a moment of weakness. She had to resist whether her heart agreed or not. It was the right thing to do and she'd been brought up to always do the right thing.

"You're welcome," she said, pulling back slightly to gaze up at him.

He leaned closer and kissed her, sharing the joy of the moment. It was as if time stood still, and she didn't want to break the contact between them.

Instead, she did the unthinkable—she kissed him back.

So much for resisting.

A buzzer sounded throughout the office, breaking them apart as they both remembered where they were and they had jobs to do.

"I'm sorry," he stammered. "I guess I got caught up in the moment."

"Me, too," Juliet said, before heading for the door. "I'll look in on Johnny and see what he needs." It would give her the chance to calm her racing heart and figure out what the kiss meant to her and what she wanted to do about it. They definitely needed to discuss what had just happened.

By the time Juliet finished helping Johnny, she eagerly returned to the office, more than ready for another conversation with the doctor.

Except he'd left.

Gone home according to Olivia—and all without saying goodbye.

Chapter Thirteen

♥

WALKING TOWARD THE CHURCH, Juliet took the time to savor the pretty flowers in bloom, to wave at the friendly neighbors in town, and gaze up at the sky. She'd spent a lot of time thinking ever since Jake's kiss but hadn't come any closer to deciding what to do about it. If there was anything to do about it considering he'd pulled another disappearing act.

The problem was she liked him. What wasn't there to like? Other than his unsocial, impersonal, gruff exterior that is. But even the gruff exterior was gone, pointing to changes she couldn't help but admire. It meant he was open to new ideas, and she couldn't help but wonder if in time, he'd even consider another relationship—and by that, she meant her, of course.

Although, his apology for the kiss before he made a swift exit without seeing her, and his continued silence since, didn't exactly confirm her line of thinking.

It was just a jubilant kiss to celebrate a successful surgery. *Doctors don't kiss nurses to celebrate*—unless they were interested in said nurse. *No.* Perhaps the kiss was done as a way to celebrate his return to medical practice. Or at least that's what she thought at the time. Except he'd left and hadn't come back. It would be interesting to see if he showed up Monday morning. And if he didn't, it would be time for her to ramp up her efforts to help him.

One day at the office was progress, but not nearly enough to call it an overwhelming success in helping him find his way back to his calling. God's calling for his life.

Juliet shook her head, trying to dispel all thoughts of Jake Kensington. She walked into the sanctuary and found a seat at the back. Several of the towns-folk waved in recognition, making her feel a part of Hollow Creek.

An older woman and her husband came and sat next to her. "Good morning, dear," the woman said. "I don't believe we've met. I'm Gilda Harrington and this is my husband, Tom." She pointed at the older man who leaned forward to wave at her, his smile equally warm and welcoming as his wife's.

"Good morning. It's nice to meet you both. I'm—"

"The new doctor in town," Gilda said with a flourish. "I've been hearing all about you."

"Not quite. I'm the nurse. I'm sure anything you've been hearing is about Dr. K," Juliet added, trying to set the record straight.

"Mrs. Trenton had a lot to say. And yes, we heard Dr. K was back, but she said you were wonderful with her boy, making him comfortable and less scared. And giving him shots. That boy don't like shots, but he sure didn't mind the pretty doctor giving him one." Gilda chuckled.

"Nurse," she corrected. It's like the town had one mode—doctors and medical centers. It was a nice thought. Flattering, in fact, but not the truth, nonetheless. "That was sweet of her. Johnny is such a sweet boy and I hope he's doing well. No ill after-effects." She didn't bother to tell the woman that Dr. K's return wasn't official. She'd just been the catalyst to force him back into the clinic for the first time. The rest was up to him—more or less.

"I don't think so, but after church, if you come to the picnic, you can see for yourself. Johnny will be there, from what I understand. But then, lots of folks in town show up for the church's picnics. Not many say no to a free meal." Gilda shot her a wink, as though it were a hush-hush secret between them.

"I'd love to come, and not just for the free food." Juliet thought it would be a good chance to meet people. And she really would like to check on Johnny's arm.

They all turned their attention to the front of the room as the praise team started to sing, their voices beautiful and powerful. She'd expected a choir, but it turned out Hollow Creek was progressive with uplifting and vibrant music, the sounds sending shivers of love and joy throughout her body.

The pastor was just as engaging, his humorous and yet real viewpoints in combining today's world and the biblical view held her enthralled. It reminded her of her father's sermons, and it made Juliet miss home a little. Ever since she could remember she'd listened to her father preach, hanging onto his every word. Pastor James' sermon really hit home when he started discussing family life and home. Except where she was thinking of her own childhood home, Pastor James was referring to families just starting out. Marriage. Life. Family. New beginnings.

Something she'd rather not think about. Most people her age already had a family and kids, or they were well on their way. *Not her.*

It didn't help as she noticed Gilda and her husband holding hands. They looked as though they'd been together all their lives and were still in love. And still in church. A significant factor in the relationship, and another confirmation of what she'd believed her entire life. Equally yoked relationships stood a better chance of survival. Not perfect, but better.

After the message, Juliet headed outside and made her way to where others were setting up the picnic area. It wasn't long before someone shoved a box of napkins in her arms.

"Do you mind spreading these out on that table?" the young man asked, pointing at the table.

"Sure thing. I'm willing to help in whatever way I'm needed." Juliet smiled and moved off to the table indicated.

"Oh, thank you, dear," an older woman spoke up as Juliet placed the stack of napkins near the plates.

"Your welcome."

"Looks like a good turnout, but then folks enjoy this sort of thing right after church. Don't believe I know you," the woman said, one eyebrow raised in question.

"I'm Juliet Walker, the new nurse at the medical center in town. Temporarily anyway," she said, extending her hand to introduce herself.

"Hi there. I'm Diane Booker, and that," she said, pointing to an older man about twenty feet away, "is my husband, Bill."

The man headed their way, a broad smile on his weathered face.

"Hey, honey. This is Juliet Walker, the new nurse in town," Diane said by way of introduction.

"Nice to meet you. Welcome to Hollow Creek," Bill said, shaking her hand.

"Thank you. I've just got to ask, how long have you two been married? You seem cozy, like so many others in church this morning. It's like you all have something in the water—like an eternal spring of love and hope or something." Hollow Creek was overflowing with couples in love and Juliet was a bit envious.

"Nah. Folks around here just like to keep things simple. Of course, the men all know the secret to a happy marriage." He grinned.

"Which is?" she asked, wondering if he would admit to what Juliet had already figured out.

"Happy wife, happy life." Bill busted out laughing as he leaned toward Diane and kissed her on the cheek.

"You're incorrigible, but right." Diane shook her head, loving her husband's teasing. "We've been married forty-six years."

"Forty-six long years," Bill said, pulling his wife close and shooting Juliet a wink.

"Wow. How wonderful! My parents have been married thirty-two and I love it when I see more happy marriages." Although his answer wasn't at all what she expected.

"What about you, dear? Are you married?" Diane asked.

She couldn't help but notice Diane's gaze drop to Juliet's left hand. "No. No husband. No boyfriends. No prospects. I think God has other plans for my life."

"Nonsense," Bill scoffed. "You're young still. Plenty of time. Maybe someone right here in Hollow Creek will catch your eye."

"I don't know. I stopped looking after the last one." Juliet shrugged.

"That's when you usually find the right one. What do you think of Dr. K? He's the town's most eligible bachelor. A little rusty, but a good man who needs a good woman. Maybe that's you," Diane offered, smiling.

"Doubtful. We work together and I'm only here temporarily." And if there was one thing she'd learned growing up, marriages didn't last if you didn't find someone in the same place you were on your spiritual journey. And as to her and Jake—well, they couldn't be any further apart on their spiritual journey.

"You never know. Hey, I've got an idea. We need someone to help with the children at the annual outdoor Shakespeare festival. The volunteer is in charge of entertaining the kids with games and crafts during the play. Weekend after next. Any chance you'd be willing to help?"

"I'd love to. I've got lots of free time on the weekends and it would give me a chance to get to know more people."

"Yes, it will. And maybe meet someone," Bill added with a wink. The man was incorrigible.

"Enough, you two." She shook her head. "I'm going to mingle and leave you two to your own fairy tale. Not everyone can have what you have." Juliet waved as she wandered off, hoping to meet more people.

They were wrong about Jake—the part where they were trying to link the two of them together.

Chapter Fourteen

♥

JULIET ARRIVED AT THE clinic early on Monday, eager to see what the day held. More specifically if Jake returned to the clinic. She couldn't wait to update him on Johnny's progress. The kid was doing great and in high spirits when she spoke to him at the picnic, and even talking about fishing again. Something mostly due to Jake's encouragement.

The overhead doorbell buzzed, and Juliet headed to the front room. "Good morning, Olivia," she said when she spotted the receptionist.

"Good morning. You're here early. What's up?" Olivia moved to sit at her desk and fired up the computer.

"Just trying to get a jump on things. Straighten up a bit. Restock the rooms," Juliet said in a rush.

Olivia stopped and looked up at her, her brow furrowing slightly. "All stuff you can do during the day. What's really going on?"

She shrugged. "Fine. I'm anxious to see if Dr. K returns today." Olivia wouldn't let the matter drop until she admitted the truth, so it was easier to get it over with.

"Why would you think that? I got the impression it was a onetime thing."

"It was just something he said." More like something he did—not that she'd be telling anyone, especially not Olivia. There was a limit to how much Juliet would reveal.

"Don't hold your breath. I was shocked you got him here in the first place. I'm sure that took some arm twisting. Or charm," Olivia added with a grin.

Juliet shook her head. "Definitely the first." Not wanting to continue the discussion, she headed through the door that led to the patient rooms.

By the time lunch rolled around, she'd seen four appointments and two drop-in patients. Unfortunately, there was no sign of Jake and she was forced to acknowledge Olivia had been right—he wasn't coming.

Juliet left the clinic, deciding she might as well finish setting up her account and bring her lunch back to the clinic. The rest of the day was surprisingly busy with back-to-back appointments, which helped to keep her mind off Jake, and the aching disappointment at bay.

At five, Olivia volunteered to close the office since Juliet had opened that morning. She didn't have to be asked twice because once she realized Jake was a no-show, Juliet had decided her next move with Jake. It was time to pay him a visit. He deserved an update on Johnny and it would provide her with an excellent excuse to see him.

Juliet turned onto the gravel road just outside of town. She slowed down, the bumps and ruts jostling her. Not to mention, she didn't want to damage the car Olivia had lent her. She'd planned on getting her own car last weekend, but Olivia's mother was away visiting her sister and the car was just sitting in her driveway. It had been a most welcome option to aid in getting around town.

She found the turnoff that headed deep into the woods and to Jake's cabin. Hopefully, he wouldn't mind an unexpected visitor, but she knew better than to call and ask permission.

Pulling up next to the barn, she hopped out of the car and glanced around, relieved when she spotted Jake's truck parked on the side of the house. Taking a deep breath, she headed for the house, awed by the beauty of the countryside views he got to experience every day. Some things about the way he lived seemed ultra-simple and ultra-peaceful, others, like the outhouse—not so much.

All Jake needed to do was to learn to combine the two worlds.

Juliet knocked on the rickety screen door. There was no answer, and no sounds coming from within. She looked around but didn't see any sign of Jake.

"Jake," she called out, pressing her face to the screen. Still no answer. She headed for the barn to check it out just in case he was working on the four-wheeler. Or, for that matter, gone on his four-wheeler. Something she hadn't thought of before.

She rounded the bend and entered the area where he parked the utility vehicle. It was there, hood up, as if he'd been working on it. But there was no sign of him. "Jake," she called again. Still no answer, but he couldn't have gone far.

Juliet headed back to the house, determined to wait for him. She went inside, knowing he never locked the cabin, and she was thirsty. Hopefully, he wouldn't mind.

Glass of water in hand, she returned to the main living area. She walked around the room, taking in the details of his life. The bookshelf caught her attention, and she moved to stand in front of it, hoping to find something of interest to keep her occupied while she waited for his return. Before, Jake had made it clear he didn't like people nosing into his business and she'd avoided all things personal.

Juliet scanned the titles, surprised to see several best-selling novels. She hadn't pegged him as an avid reader, but his collection was something almost any reader would be able to find something to enjoy. She continued to scan the shelves, trying to decide which one to pick. Down at the bottom, there were several large albums stacked and shoved out of the way.

She felt a little guilty as she started to pull one out, but they were in plain sight, and her curiosity was piqued. Juliet shot a quick look at the front door, but there was no sign of Jake. Just a quick peek, she promised herself.

The album was wedged in tight, and she gave it a tug. When it came free, an old Bible fell to the ground. Juliet picked it up reverently, in total shock as Jake owned one. Hoping it would give her insight to the man Jake once was, she opened the front cover and read the dedication.

Sophia Kensington. Where had she heard that name? His mother? No. His wife. Juliet sucked in a deep breath. His wife's Bible. It was the last thing she needed to be caught with if Jake came back. Juliet squatted, intent on shoving both items back where they belonged.

A picture and a card fell out on the floor, and as she retrieved them, she couldn't help seeing the picture. It was the same woman as the photo in Jake's room. Sophia was a young, beautiful woman, her long dark hair framing her laughing face as she looked up into the eyes of Jake as he held her in his arms. The picture had captured the full essence of a smiling man gazing down at the woman he loved, not caring who noticed.

Lucky woman. The thought came out of nowhere. She shoved it aside, instead focusing on the card she held. The wedding invitation was dated for almost three years ago. True love cut short. It was such a tragic story.

A scuffle on the front porch alerted her Jake had returned. She shoved the objects back into place, but it was a tight fit and she didn't want to damage the precious piece of history.

"Give me those," Jake's voice boomed from the doorway. "What are you doing here?" He crossed the room in only a couple of strides and snatched the books from her hands, his expression one of barely concealed anger.

Caught red-handed, there was no excuse good enough. "I...I...I'm sorry," she mumbled.

"It's past time you left."

She'd never seen Jake this angry. "Listen, I really wasn't trying to pry. It's not exactly hidden, and I was just looking to find something to read while I waited for you to return."

"I didn't ask for you to visit. Say what you wanted to say and leave." She noticed Jake was clutching both books to his chest as if forming a barrier between them.

Juliet took a step toward him instead of retreating. "I said I was sorry. I came by to give you news about Johnny." She had to find a way to connect with him and slow down his assumptions before he went too far in his accusations.

His eyes flared when he heard the boy's name. "How is he?" Jake asked, just as she'd known he would. A doctor can't resist status updates on their patients.

"He's doing great." She smiled. "He was hoping to see you at the church picnic on Sunday, but since you weren't there, he told me to tell you thanks. And that he was looking forward to his next fishing trip."

"Yeah, you know I don't do social stuff anymore. But that's great about Johnny."

"There's more to his message."

"More?"

"He's hoping you'll go with him on the next fishing trip since it was you who talked him into not giving it up." Not that she expected him to accept, but coming from Johnny, it was worth a shot.

"I can't."

"Says who? I'm sure you have a fishing pole. It's just a couple of hours of your time. Surely, you can do it for Johnny, if not for yourself. You need to get out more. Seriously."

"Are you done, preacher woman?" His tone had grown softer, the corners of his mouth relaxing from the fierce set of his jaw of only moments ago.

"Not preaching. I'll leave that to the pastor—and my father. It was just a friendly suggestion."

Jake nodded. "Duly noted. Does that mean you had one of those preachy fathers?"

"No." She laughed, grateful for the ease of tension between them. Which was a good thing, considering her intentions in coming here hadn't been to ruin all her efforts to help him. "I have one of those pastor fathers. It was mostly good. Higher expectations, yes, but a tremendous amount of love."

"I see. In other words, spoiled. Is that why you don't take no for an answer?"

"Maybe. But also because I like you, Jake Kensington. As a friend," she rushed to add, thinking it sounded more like she was pouring her heart out to him—which she wasn't.

He shook his head. "I don't know why."

"Because you've got a big heart, you're talented, mostly smart, eager to help others—"

"Mostly smart? What's that supposed to mean?" Jake asked, frowning.

"*Mostly* because you left the practice and didn't return. It's time to move forward with your life. I'm really sorry about your wife, but you can't run away from who you are forever." She knew when to press forward and when to retreat and he'd given her a golden press-forward moment.

"You don't understand," he said, moving to set the books on the table and out of his sight and turning away from them.

"Maybe I don't because everyone's journey is different. But I do know hiding out here won't bring her back. You were in your element on Friday—I watched you. You can't deny there was a spark of life in you that hadn't been there until you picked up the scalpel and went to work. I almost got the impression you wanted to come back; what changed your mind?"

"It was all from the rush of a successful procedure. There's a high of knowing you helped someone. That's all it was. Joy to help Johnny, but it was just one moment. Not the future."

"And the kiss?" Juliet decided to go for the jugular.

Jake winced. "Was a result of the joy. That's all."

"Good. I was worried that might be what was keeping you from coming back—but you have nothing to worry about from me."

"That's good to know, but why do you say it like that? It's not very flattering." He gazed at her, a frown deepening on his face.

"I didn't realize you needed flattery," Juliet said with a chuckle.

"I don't. Forget I asked. Since you're not going to let it go, I'll tell you why I won't go back. Maybe then you'll leave me alone." He moved to the couch to sit down, and she followed.

"Fat chance, but try me."

"I fell in love with my wife in high school. Sophia was my everything. She stuck by me through all my medical schooling and waited out my dream to become a doctor. We were married shortly after I finished my residency. She even gave up her roots here in Hollow Creek to move to the city with me. When the time was right, we moved back, and I opened a practice here. But then she got sick."

Juliet's smile disappeared, realizing the dark cloud hanging above Jake's head was about to show its true colors. "I'm sorry. What happened?" Asking about Sophia was hard, but she wanted to help.

"It was the influenza. She kept saying it was just a cold. But then she got worse. I came home from work one day and she had a high fever and was shaking. I took her to the hospital in Gatlinburg, but we didn't get there in time for them to be able to save her. Her lungs and heart simply gave out under the strain."

Juliet took his hand. "Jake, it's heartbreaking to lose someone you love, but it's not enough reason to walk away from medicine. Sophia wouldn't have wanted you to give up your dreams because of her death."

He yanked his hand away. "But what of her dreams? I put off having a family because of medical school, always waiting for the right time. I denied her of her dream."

"But it wasn't your fault."

"That's where you're wrong. It was my fault. I should have recognized the signs. Paid better attention. She had undetected heart disease and needed antiviral drugs, not antibiotics. If she had gotten to the hospital sooner, she wouldn't have died. It was too much strain on her heart, and the influenza had caused pneumonia and then respiratory failure. She died in my arms."

"You're a doctor, not God. You can't know or control everything. God called her home. To a better place. She wouldn't have wanted this for you," she said, pointing around the cabin. "Living like a recluse and ignoring your God-given talents. Talents she supported you in every step of the way. The real tragedy is you walking away from what you both worked hard to achieve. She was a part of that journey with you every step of the way."

"You don't pull any punches, do you? Here's the kicker you don't know, Miss-Fix-It; I may have been the one who brought the virus home," Jake said, his head and shoulders dropping forward in defeat.

He truly felt responsible for Sophia's death, just as Olivia had warned her. It was a great burden to carry.

"Honestly, it wouldn't change anything. But what if you didn't? Quit beating yourself up for something you had no control over. This is the reason you over-reacted when I was sick, isn't it?" She slapped herself up against the side of her head. "This totally explains why you were so overbearing and hard to deal with. It's not that you're a hard-hearted recluse, it's that you have a loving heart that's been deeply hurt. The rest is just a cover."

"Don't get carried away. It doesn't change anything. I can't go back, even if I wanted to."

"Why?"

"You ask too many questions. I bared my soul to you, so let's leave it alone. Please?"

"Fine. For now," she said, patting him on the arm. "If I see Johnny, I'll tell him you're looking forward to fishing with him."

"Juliet, I didn't say that."

"No, but if you want me to leave..."

"Fine. For your information, I do like to fish. Or I did. I haven't done any fishing since long before medical school."

"It sounds like this is the perfect time to do it again. Maybe you'll find exactly what you've been missing. Talk to you later, Jake. Maybe you could join me at church on Sunday?"

"Don't press your luck." Jake smiled and shook his head, resigned to the fact he was going fishing, but unwilling to give another inch.

But Juliet was unwilling to back down from the challenge.

Chapter Fifteen

♥

J ULIET AND OLIVIA LOOKED up from the computer as the overhead doorbell buzzed when the front door opened, Juliet straightening when she noticed it was Jake. It had been two days since they'd last spoke and at last, her prayers were answered.

"Well, hello, Dr. K. We were hoping you'd show up sooner than later," Olivia said, refuting her claim yesterday that she didn't expect him to show up at all.

"Don't get too excited. I'm not here to stay. I need to go over some things with Juliet." Jake looked good. Comfortable. Too comfortable since he was missing his white clinic coat. He wasn't here to work.

"Well, of course she's here. She's a dedicated professional. Place needs more of them. When are you coming back? Everyone in town is talking about it." Olivia lifted her chin and glared at him, daring him to contradict her.

"I'm not. One day to help in an emergency situation doesn't change a thing. You can squash the rumors anytime," Jake said, pinning the receptionist with a glare as if to tell her to butt out.

"Such a shame," Olivia said, ignoring his warning and not pulling any punches when it came to stating facts. *Or opinions.*

"What did you need to talk to me about?" Juliet was more than a little curious if his presence didn't involve his return to the office. Hopefully, it would be something that would give her another opportunity to work on Project Return for Jake.

"I wanted to let you know that although I appreciate your input and concern, I can't return to the clinic and practice medicine. Therefore, I've reposted the open position for a doctor, significantly increasing the benefits and salary in the hopes of attracting someone with excellent experience and staying power."

"Apparently, you didn't think enough about what I said. Jake, this isn't the right decision and you know it. It's time," she said, lowering her voice.

"You're wrong. I did, however, set it up so that you could review the applications from the Sunshine Employment Agency as they come in and make sure the candidate is someone that meets with your approval. It's important to have a cohesive medical team and since you're half of it, you should have the biggest input."

"Except I'm not here to stay. And what are we supposed to do in the meantime? What if something worse happens to someone in town and there's no one here qualified to help? We had time to get you here with Johnny—we might not be so lucky with another patient."

"Let's just hope it doesn't happen. Hollow Creek is a quiet town."

Not exactly the answer she wanted to hear. "That's not good enough."

"What's that supposed to mean?"

"I'll agree to stay until someone takes the job and I'll look over the applications, but only if you agree to return to the clinic until the position is filled and the new doctor takes up residence." She was going to push the limits with Jake. One thing she'd learned for sure about him was that he cared about the practice, and more importantly, he cared about the people in town. "And you agree to go to church with me." Might as well go all the way while she had him in a tight spot.

"Juliet—"

"Deal or no deal? You don't have a choice if you want me to stay. I'm not working in an environment that I can't give my patients the best of what they deserve."

Jake rubbed the back of his neck, clearly not liking the direction the conversation had turned. "This is blackmail." He let out a deep breath. "No church, and you have yourself a deal. I'm pretty sure the sizable salary will manage to attract someone in short order."

"One church visit." The art of compromise was her strong suit—Jake just hadn't known it before he began negotiations. On a high note, he was negotiating, which meant she had him right where she wanted-ed.

"Fine. One visit. See you in the morning. I've got things to attend to today in order to meet your demands." Jake turned and walked out of the office.

Juliet glanced at Olivia, noting the woman was grinning like the Cheshire cat after a bowl of cream. "Smooth work, Juliet. I do believe you have that man's number. It's about time someone else did."

"Someone else?" She hated to ask but couldn't stop herself.

"Someone other than his late wife."

"Oh, but that's not what this is about."

"But it could be. I've been telling you to stay and that the town needs you, but I reckon there's a good chance the doc does too." Olivia gazed intently at her, waiting to see her reaction. Juliet wouldn't give the woman the satisfaction of thinking she'd figured out some grand behind-the-scenes romance.

"Olivia, it's not like that. This is temporary for me and you know it. I have a job back home."

Olivia shrugged. "And you have a job here, one that's been offered full-time to my recollection."

Juliet did recollect, and it was part of her confusion. She'd thought about it over and over and still had no clear answer as to whether Hollow Creek was a new door God was opening and where he wanted her to stay, or if it was a temporary stopover. God would reveal his plan eventually and until then, she'd just have to wait.

Realizing what had just happened, Juliet smiled. Not only had Jake agreed to return to the office, but he was also coming to church. *Once.* She was only the catalyst to open his heart up to the world and his faith again. The rest was up to him—and God.

"Let me get to work and see what I can do to fill the scheduling slots. Lots of folks gonna want to be seen knowing Dr. K is back in the office. I'm not planning on advertising the temporary part, and I suggest you do the same. Otherwise, we'll be buried alive in the sea of patients catching up on medical care before he takes flight again."

"Okay, works for me." Juliet smiled and headed for the office. Her first order of business was to clear out of his office and move next door to the smaller office.

In between patients and moving things, it took her long into the night, but by morning, she had the

Wi-Fi hotspot set up and her own laptop connected to the office's mainframe unit in order to keep up with what was happening. Olivia managed the emails, but patients' notes were her responsibility and she wanted to be prepared.

Not to mention, she had to filter through the applications the agency sent over. It wasn't a task she was eager to do, but Jake had been right. It meant a lot that he trusted her to pick the new doctor, even if it was for all the wrong reasons. He still thought she'd change her mind and stay.

The replacement would need to be someone like Jake. Easy going, smart, and calm under fire, and someone who would love the community as much as he did. He might be a reclusive now, but it was clear in every aspect of the clinic, that nothing had been too good for Hollow Creek.

By the time Juliet returned the next morning, it felt as though she hadn't left. It might have been easier to sleep on the couch in Jake's office, but then the idea of him coming in early and finding her had been enough to make her head home.

The door to the clinic was already unlocked, Olivia beating her here. Juliet hoped the coffee was ready as well, as she was in dire need of some strong brew. The front room was empty, and she headed for the back offices.

"Olivia," she called out, spotting the coffeepot in the corner, the fresh aroma wafting toward her. Juliet moved to pour a cup.

"Good morning," Jake said from behind her.

She spun around and was unprepared for the sight that greeted her. "Good morning," she managed to get the words out while her brain malfunctioned.

Jake Kensington looked mighty fine. Clean cut, dress slacks, a button-down dress shirt, and a doctor's lab coat. All very professional and very handsome—a single woman's ideal man. "Hope you like the way I made the coffee. Thought I'd get here early and go over today's files. Do you have them?"

Juliet swallowed, trying to regroup. "I do. They're on my desk. I'll get them."

"You didn't have to move out of this office. I won't be here long."

"Long enough that we didn't need to share the space that's rightfully yours." She left the room, returning moments later with the pile of patient folders. "There might be more coming. Olivia put the word out yesterday you were returning, and the phone was ringing off the hook with appointments the rest of the day."

"That's fine. They'll all find out soon enough that it's not for long. At least this way, everyone has a chance to be seen. Any applications come through yet for the position?"

"It's been less than twenty-four hours," she said, shaking her head. "But I'll check while you look these over." Juliet rolled her eyes and started out the door.

"Thank you." His gravelly voice warmed her. Jake didn't want to be here, but clearly, he was going to make the best of it. She hoped he did the same when it came time to go to church.

Juliet sat at her desk and typed in the password on her computer. She sipped her coffee while she waited for the office program to load. After clicking on the tab for online job postings, she was more than a little surprised to see three applications already there for review.

Jake had been right; whatever salary he was offering was attractive enough to make Hollow Creek a new career destination. One by one, she went through each application. One by one, she was less satisfied with the applicant than the one before. Sure, they were all qualified. That was a no-brainer. But as she read their letters of intent and interest, none held the easy-going passion she was looking for in a candidate. None were like Jake.

And therein lay the problem. Juliet wanted Jake to return to practice, and it was obvious to her he was the perfect person for the clinic. The problem was convincing him to stay, and with applications rolling in, she wouldn't have long to do it.

Juliet sat there staring at the screen, trying to figure out how to stall the inevitable. A new doctor. What she needed was time for Jake to get back into the swing of things and change his mind. She returned to the first applicant and hit reply, trying to decide what to say. Suddenly, she knew exactly what to do. Jake would be furious, but technically, the position

had already been filled. They had a doctor in residence.

She penned out a standard *thank you for your interest, but the position has been filled* letter and pasted it into the reply box. She hesitated only a second before pressing send, and then did the same with the other two applications before she reconsidered. Pulling up the agency account, she deleted the entries off the server as though they'd never existed. This way, Jake would never know the difference.

It was for his own good.

Chapter Sixteen

♥

JAKE WALKED INTO JULIETTE'S office, a frown on his face. They'd been working together for a week and the place had run with smooth efficiency, as if they'd worked together for years. Sunday, of course, she'd given him a pass when he bailed on going to church, but then he had a good reason. A patient house-call.

"What's up? You aren't smiling. Did I forget to restock the bandages or hand sanitizer?" she teased.

"You know better than that. You are nothing but efficient, and you know it. But it's been a week and you haven't said anything about the responses to the employment ad. I would have thought by now we'd have quite a few takers. So, what's the problem? Is it no applications are coming in, or are the people not qualified, or is it that they don't meet up with your expectations?"

"It's the same thing I've been telling you every day when you ask. I'm not seeing what this office needs." It was the only hedge answer she could give since she wouldn't lie. Jake was what the office needed; therefore, no other applicant would work.

"Fine. I'll talk to the agency if nothing happens over the weekend. I had lofty hopes that are quickly diminishing. Maybe the doctors coming out of medical school simply have no interest in a small-town practice because they have to pay for the big-city schools they attended and owe hundreds of thousands of dollars."

Juliet would have to nix the idea and come up with a better plan before Monday. "I'm out of here," she said, pulling on a light sweater for her walk home.

Jake glanced at his watch. "Hot date on a Friday night? You normally stick around at least an hour after closing time working on the daily files and catching up notes."

"No, only tired. Once word got out you were in the office, this place has doubled its business."

"I guess that's a good thing." He chuckled. "I need to increase the revenues to pay for two medical staffers."

Juliet smiled. "One. I'm temporary. And don't forget your promise to meet me at church. Since it's unlikely you'll have another house call excuse, I'll be out front waiting at eight forty-five on Sunday."

"Still going to hold me to that, huh?" He grimaced. "I was hoping—"

"Be there," she said firmly, not willing to give an inch on the promise he made. "Have a nice night." She waved as she walked out the front door, leaving him standing there, shaking his head.

Sunday morning rolled around far quicker than Juliet expected. She put on a pretty blue dress with white flowers that she'd picked up at the five and dime in town. Staying longer than she planned, or for that matter staying at all, her wardrobe had been woefully ill-equipped to handle the extra load. As a result, she'd been forced to go shopping and spend money on new clothes she'd never wear again. Luckily, her roommate had boxed up some things and mailed them, otherwise the limited choices in town might have left her hanging out at the laundry mat.

She waited outside in front of the church and checked her watch. At two minutes to the start of the service, Juliet was ready to admit the truth—Jake wasn't coming. Turning to go inside, she couldn't help the sense of disappointment washing over her.

A lone figure came around the corner of the church dressed in jeans, a polo shirt, and boots. *Jake.*

Several people stopped to talk to him, several more waved and continued inside, eager to claim their regular seat for the sermon.

When he finally made it to her side, they only had minutes to spare.

"Good morning. I'm so glad you made it," she said, smiling up at him.

"Good morning. I like to think I keep all my promises. To not keep them makes one a liar. Something I can't abide."

Ouch. Did he know? Or was he just making a point? "Shall we go in?" she asked.

They found seats at the back of the room. Juliet hadn't missed the odd looks she and Dr. K drew as they entered the church together. Several people recognized her and waved, but most were paying attention to Jake. The outpouring of kindness since she'd decided to stay in Hollow Creek continued to make her feel welcome and at home.

Juliet pointed to the stage where the praise team prepared to start their worship. "I love the music on Sunday mornings," she whispered, gazing up at Jake.

His face was lined with tension, veins popping on his forehead. One hand went to his face as he brushed his palm over the skin, rubbing it as if trying to erase something. A memory?

She reached for his hand, sensing his distress. The sweet sounds of music filled the air. "I just love the music. It's so uplifting," she said, leaning close and repeating the words since he hadn't answered. Anything to draw him out of wherever he'd gone in his head.

"I agree. It's different from what I remember when I used to come here."

"Did you come often?" she asked, hoping for some insight as to what was bothering him.

"I did." He nodded. "Weekly."

"I would have never guessed. The music at our church back home has been this band style for quite a while. My father believes it's a great way to reach out to the younger generation. It definitely works. The place is packed every Sunday."

"Looks to be working here as well. I don't remember it being this full. What was it like growing up as the preacher's daughter?" he asked as the music came to a stop and they prepared to transition to the message part of the service.

"Not easy. Part of me rebelled, part of me embraced. As I got older, I made my own decision to follow God and accepted Jesus into my heart. It wasn't until then that I truly understood."

The pastor approached the podium, and the room fell into silence. The morning message was focused on why terrible things happened to good people and Juliet could feel the tension radiating from Jake. She was worried the message was too much for his first time back. It's not like she had any control over the content—but God did.

Jake suddenly stood, and without a word, turned and walked out. The message had struck a nerve in Jake, and Juliet needed to trust that God knew exactly how much Jake could handle.

Juliet wasn't sure whether to follow or let him have some space. She thought about it a minute, mulling over his admission he'd gone to church regularly. It closed the wide gap between them, opening her brain up to the what-ifs of a relationship. It was a foolish what-if, however, given his current state of grief for his late wife, not to mention his current non-relationship with God. Just coming to church was a hardship for him.

Her thoughts drifted to the situation at work. More specifically, her duplicity. It wasn't like her and the longer it went on, the more she was determined to fess up. Maybe it was the impact of being closer to God in this moment, but the conviction laid on her heart told her exactly what she needed to do. And right after the service, she'd find him and set the record straight. He'd be upset with her, but it was a chance she had to take.

Better yet, tell him now. If she could help him through whatever he was dealing with and tell him the truth, it might help push them into a new place of trust. *Or destroy it completely.*

Outside, she caught up with him, grabbing his arm. "Are you okay? Is there anything I can do to help?" she asked, her heart aching for the man who hadn't let go, grief etched on his face, and clearly still controlling his life.

"I don't need your help, Juliet. You've done enough. I showed up at church just like we agreed. You didn't specify how long I had to stay."

"But where are you going? I'd like a chance to talk to you." Now wasn't the time, judging by his anguish, but she was trying anything to keep him from leaving, worried and wanting to help.

"Not now, Juliet." Jake pulled away and walked off down the sidewalk. He paused, turning in through the wrought-iron gates just past the church parking lot.

The cemetery.

Juliet knew exactly where Jake was going and why. He was in a dark place and Juliet had been a fool to think she could help him. Her lofty ideals did nothing to ease his pain. Maybe she'd been too pushy, making him a project because of what was missing in her own life. In trying to find something to validate her reason for being, she'd crossed some lines.

Jake's faith journey was between him and God, and the only thing she could do was pray.

The truth hit her hard. Praying was something she could do from the city. And if she left, Jake would be forced to work at the clinic and become self-reliant. He'd enjoyed this past week. How much better would it be for him to experience it alone? Being needed and trusted by the community would go a long way to help heal his pain and for him to realize the town trusted him and wanted him back. He was one of them.

Far be it for her to stand in the way of Jake's healing if that was how God could reach him. And if it meant leaving Hollow Creek, she'd do it.

Chapter Seventeen

♥

Hollow Creek Medical Center

Dear Dr. Kensington,

I regret to inform you that I must return to Memphis and will be unable to remain working in the temporary position of RN at the Medical Center. This decision has not been easily made but is unavoidable. I appreciate the opportunity and wish you the very best in not only your medical future, but your personal future as well.

With your return to the clinic, I have every belief you can manage the caseload single-handedly and feel confident the people of Hollow Creek are in expert hands. I will stay through the end of this week as I've promised to help at the Shakespeare festival this weekend. If you feel the need for an assistant, perhaps you could advertise for one.

Thanks again for everything.

Sincerely,

Juliet Walker

Juliet felt another twinge of guilt about the applications she'd deleted. More like a gut-wrenching guilt, but guilt was guilt. It meant she'd done something wrong, and she knew it. No matter how she tried to sugarcoat her response to his daily questions, she'd not told the whole truth. She'd tried to control the outcome of the future and only managed to make things worse—for Jake.

Someone she'd come to care about far more than she should have, and the very reason it was time to turn tail and run. Jake was a man who loved his late wife, and she'd been a fool to let her imagination run away from her after the kiss. Juliet was the third and unwanted wheel. She'd gone and done it again, falling for a man unequally yoked and, worse still, emotionally unavailable.

It wasn't long before her email notification pinged. Juliet knew without looking it would be Jake's answer.

Dear Juliet Walker,

I was sorry to receive your resignation letter and hate to see you leave, but I respect your decision. Hollow Creek is a small town, so don't worry about working this week. As you said, I can handle the workload.

I apologize for my gruffness this morning and hope it had nothing to do with your decision.

Sincerely,

Dr. Jake Kensington

Chapter Eighteen

♥

WALKING INTO THE OFFICE earlier than usual, Juliet was hoping to collect her things before Olivia showed up. It wouldn't be easy telling her new friend why she was leaving. No one would understand even if she tried to explain it, which she preferred not to do. It stung that Jake hadn't even wanted her here this week. It was as though their friendship had meant nothing up to this point.

Unfortunately, luck wasn't on her side. The lights were on in the lobby, which meant Olivia was already here. So much for her pack and run idea.

"Good morning, Juliet. You're in early," Olivia said, smiling as she prepared the pot of coffee in the breakroom.

"Good morning to you, too. I...umm...there's no easy way to tell you this—"

"She's leaving," Jake said from the doorway.

Juliet hadn't anticipated him being there.

"What do you mean *leaving*?" Olivia frowned, looking back and forth between the two of them.

"Just what it sounds like," Jake said, his voice rife with tension.

"I don't know what's going on between you two, but fix it fast. Mrs. Trenton wants you to look at Johnny's arm and she's on her way in. She thinks it might be infected. And I've two more physicals set up for this morning. And a full calendar of appointments this afternoon."

Jake smiled. Not the kind of smile that suggested he was happy, quite the opposite. "That's great. Let's hope not too many at once, since it's just me now."

Olivia's eyes darkened. "You keep saying that. Where are you going?" she asked, turning to Juliet.

"She quit," Jake answered for her.

"No way. Juliet?" Olivia looked for confirmation. The woman's face held an expression of confusion and disbelief, all rolled into one.

Juliet got up the courage to finish what Jake had started. "It's true."

"Why? That's not like you. And without notice? What did you do, Jake Kensington?" Olivia turned her full outrage on Jake without having all the information.

"He didn't do anything. I've decided it's time to return to my job in the city," Juliet said, trying to smooth things over.

"Hogwash."

"It's true. But for the record, I offered to work out the week, but Dr. Kensington didn't feel it was necessary." It still stung that he'd rejected her offer and the sarcasm that laced her voice as she stated the truth was more than a little evident, but unavoidable.

"I hope you didn't say it in so many words. Clearly, you're still a little rough around the edges, having spent so much time in isolation."

"As a matter of fact, I was nice about it. I think my words were something like I *could manage it.*" That's not how Juliet remembered it.

"*Hmmph.* So, what did you do to run her off?" Olivia stood there, arms crossed and demanding answers.

"Why would it have anything to do with me?" Jake asked, scowling.

"Because she loves it here. We've talked and I know things. This is too sudden."

It was time to let Jake off the hook. "Olivia, I can speak for myself. I'm not leaving because of anything Jake's done. It's just time. Trust me on this. I'll be at the Shakespeare festival on Sunday to help out with the kids, so there is that."

Olivia huffed. "Men."

"What's that supposed to mean?" Jake asked.

"If you can't see what's in front of your face, you're not as smart as I thought you were."

"And what's that?" he asked, his expression one of complete bafflement. Juliet felt sorry for him, but there wasn't anything she could say to change Olivia's mind.

"She cares about you. Any fool can see the way she watches you when she knows you're not looking."

"Olivia! Stop with this nonsense," Juliet exclaimed, her heart racing as Olivia's pronouncement hung in the air with electrifying intensity. "Jake, she's talking out of turn, I promise."

"I'll be back in an hour. It'll give you time to pack and me to get out of your way," Jake said, before turning to leave. The door shut firmly behind him.

"This is nonsense. Any fool can see what's between you two. Why deny it?" Olivia asked, her friend desperately trying to stop the train that had derailed.

"Because this is not my life. And Jake's not meant to be my guy. Some things aren't meant to be. I'm sorry, Olivia. You thought wrong when you lumped us together as a couple."

Juliet left to pack her things, not wanting to discuss it anymore. *Any of it.*

Hours later, back in her room, her email notification pinged. Juliet pulled out her phone, the sender's name causing her to suck in a deep breath.

Jake Kensington.

Dear Juliet,

I'm sorry for some of the things I've said. Please reconsider staying at the Medical Center. I haven't actually told you this, but I want you to stay. I enjoyed working with you last week and would like to see where this team/friendship can go. Let me know why you're leaving, and I'll see what I can do to help. You've done so much for me, it's the least I can do. I've said from the start I wanted you to stay on permanently. I still wish you would.

Sincerely,

Dr. Jake Kensington

Somewhat mollified by his apology, Juliet tried not to think of anything else. Because thinking would get her into trouble. Jake was acting like he cared, but they'd gone down this road once before.

Nothing had changed. He was still in love with his late wife and the only way to keep him working at the clinic was to give him time to fall in love with medicine all over again. Something he couldn't do if Juliet was there and he hired another doctor.

She spent the rest of the day working out the details of getting home and walking around town, taking pictures to help her remember the place. She'd be back this weekend for the play, but her heart already recognized the goodbye. And other than Olivia stopping by her place and grilling her about why she was leaving and helping her to get squared away at the bus station, it had been a quiet day.

Dr. Kensington was back in full swing and without her help. Juliet would like to think she had a hand in his return, but she'd also come to realize if he hadn't been ready, it wouldn't have happened. Jake's return was largely due to his heart and passion for medicine. And it was the same heart and passion God would tap into, in order to make Jake's heart whole again.

She also knew it was a fool's errand to have fallen for Jake, but it had happened anyway. Part of her had hoped he'd come talk to her, but there'd been no word from him. Which, in the end, was exactly as things were intended. But if that was true, why did it hurt so much? It was a good thing she was a nurse because duty called—it was time to nurse her own broken heart.

Chapter Nineteen

J ULIET RETURNED TO WORK at the hospital in Memphis on Wednesday, but after three days, she still hadn't managed to get back into the groove. Her heart wasn't into it after Jake's last email the night she returned home. She'd read it a hundred times, and the words were now stuck in her head.

Juliet,

After I sent an email to the owner of the Sunshine Employment Agency trying to understand why no applications have been received, I discovered your duplicity and can't begin to tell you how disappointed I am. I trusted you and you abused that trust. How dare you play God with my life?

I thought you cared about me and that we were friends. I thought we shared a connection, but I realize now it was all in my head. Was I just a project for you? Someone to fix and then go on about your merry way to help the next poor unfortunate soul.

You'll be happy to know the application pool is alive and well—for both positions. Doctor and nurse.

Dr. Jake Kensington

Jake had every right to be furious with her. She was guilty of making him into a project, as though she had a gift and a duty to give him back his life. Who was she kidding? It was presumptuous of her to think she'd been led to help Jake. All it had done was make him angry.

Of course, she hadn't bothered to respond. Everything she'd done had been to make her feel useful and needed. That she had a purpose. In the end, she only proved herself a failure at something else and that she'd been wrong to decide what God's purpose was for her life, like she had any control over the outcome. Only God knew the plan and she needed to learn patience.

The truth was hard to bear, but in humility, she would work on herself and not others. Helping others was wonderful, but not if her own reasoning was to fulfill a project need inside her. Her heart had to be for others and helping a joy purely for the happiness she brought others with no expectation of reward to herself for her good deeds.

Starting with this weekend. She'd give anything not to go, but a promise was a promise and she'd do it for the children and for her friends in Hollow Creek. They say time heals hurts, and for that reason, she wanted time to pass quickly.

At least there was very little opportunity of running into Jake at the play, almost positive Grizzly Jake was on the return end of the story.

Driving toward Hollow Creek Friday after work, she made good time, but being alone with her thoughts gave her far too much time to think about her mistakes. Juliet drove past the clinic, wishing she could stop in and see Olivia. Her friend had emailed her a few times, but so far Juliet had kept her responses limited, not sure what Olivia thought of her now that she'd split town. She wasn't sure if Jake would have shared the truth or not about the application deceit.

Jake's old truck was nowhere to be seen and Juliet made a split-second decision, pulling a U-turn, and parking in front of the office.

"Hey, there," Juliet said, going through the front door. She glanced around to make sure there was no sign of any patients. *Or Jake.*

"Hey, stranger. Am I ever glad to see you." Olivia came around the desk and gave her a hug.

"Likewise. Sorry, I didn't answer your emails. I was hoping to see you when I came into town this weekend for the play."

"That's great you came back for it."

"I promised to entertain the kids. Besides, I've never been to an outdoor play and want to see what the excitement is all about," she said, grinning. There was no reason to let Olivia in on her heartache issues.

"Well, this is even better." Olivia reached into her desk and pulled out a piece of paper. "Here. Fill this out and leave it with me."

"What is it?"

"An application for the APRN position here at the clinic. Dr. K is hiring a full-time APRN."

"That's sweet, but I'm not sure it's such a good idea. I messed up while I was here, and he had every right to be angry with me. I'm sorry I didn't tell you about the behind-the-scenes things I was doing trying to help him."

"You mean about the applications? I knew. Who do you think removed the deleted email file?" Olivia grinned.

"But you didn't say anything."

"I didn't want to. You were on the right track and the first person that seem to be able to reach the man. Who am I to judge your methods with the success you were having?"

"Jake. He wasn't impressed."

"That's where you're wrong. Maybe it stung a bit when he found out, but you two were a good team. In and out of the office, if you know what I mean. You should come back. Judging by the one email you sent me, you aren't quite yourself either. Perhaps it has more to do with Dr. K than you're willing to admit."

Juliet knew this was a dangerous path to contin-ue down, and she needed to put an end to Olivia's fanciful wishful thinking. If she allowed herself to believe, it would only lead to hurt, and she'd been down that road before. "That's where you're wrong. Jake has strong opinions about relationships and his late wife. And me, and not in a good way."

Olivia's grin only deepened. "Now see, that's what I mean. You are giving me reasons why Dr. K wouldn't be in a relationship, not that you don't feel anything for him. But then, I watched you working with him and couldn't miss the way you both connected. He feels the same. I just know it."

Juliet knew she'd lost the battle. She was never good at hiding her feelings. "Was it that obvious?"

"To me it was," Olivia said, a wide grin on her face.

"Have you told him how you feel?" The idea of him knowing was more than she could bear.

"It wouldn't do any good, so please, don't say anything more. Once was enough," Juliet said, remembering the mortification she felt the last time Olivia tried to tell Jake she liked him. Juliet felt her face flushing red.

"Just think about applying, will you? What can it hurt?"

Juliet took the application and shoved it into her purse. "Fine. I'll think about it. Any chance you're free for lunch tomorrow?"

"I'd love it."

"I'll text you what time in the morning. Have a great night."

Juliet headed out the door and walked the short distance to the diner. Having missed lunch, she was eager for an almost home-cooked meal. She was surprised to run into Diane, especially without her husband close-by.

"Sit down. I'd love some company for dinner," Diane said, pointing to the seat across from her.

Juliet slid into the booth. "Everything okay? I don't see you and Bill apart very often. I thought you two were attached at the hip," she teased the older woman.

"He's at a small-group meeting and I thought I'd treat myself out to dinner."

"I see. I should have guessed it was something like that. You two have the perfect marriage."

"No marriage is perfect, mark my words. Two people who care about each other will try to work things out. That's the closest you get to perfect." She shook her head and chuckled.

"It helps that you're both in church and have the same beliefs. I've seen it with my parents. Shows the importance of finding the right person to marry in the first place."

"It wasn't always this way, dear. Bill was involved with the church, but I wasn't. I believed in God, but that's as far as it went. But over time, Bill led me to understand what I was missing out on in not having a personal relationship with the Lord. It changes a person's perspective on a lot of things. But if Bill had disregarded me in the first place because of my inequality when it came to faith, we wouldn't have what we have today. I'm glad he put *his* faith in God *and* in me. God can use people in life to help others heal and grow and love. Maybe that's your purpose with regards to Dr. K."

Juliet was shocked into silence, trying to figure out how to respond. It would almost seem as though everyone else knew before she had. "I once used to think so. I now consider it arrogance on my part. But how did you know?" There was no sense in denying the truth, even if it was too late.

"It's obvious to anyone looking. Trust me. The light in your eyes shines brighter every time that man is around. He hasn't been quite himself since you left, you know." Diane's comment reminded her about something Olivia said that she'd forgotten to ask her what she meant. *You aren't quite yourself either.*

Was it possible Jake still cared and his email was a cover? "I didn't know," Olivia said. In fact, it was almost impossible to believe.

The truth hit her like a bolt of lightning. The doctor needed a nurse. And Juliet knew one who might be right for the job. Jake might not ever be ready for a relationship, but the two did make a good team. And working with him and being friends was a whole lot better than being in another state and wondering about him. And maybe someday, he would be ready for more than friendship. If that happened, Juliet would be waiting because the truth was, she loved him. And that made him worth waiting for.

They weren't equally yoked, but they were in the same pan. Diane was right. It wasn't for Juliet to decide with who or when she'd fall in love. All she ever needed to do was listen to her heart and trust God. And what He was showing her with blinding clarity was that Jake was the man for her.

Chapter Twenty

LONG INTO THE NIGHT, Juliet mulled over the conversation at dinner with Diane and Olivia's earlier comment. They were way off base about Jake, but not about her. The question that plagued her was a simple one—what if they were right? She prayed about it until she fell asleep.

By morning, she knew what she needed to do.

Open the door. The images in her dreams were clear, and she'd put on her humility cloak and fight for more than just her job. She'd fight for Jake.

Yes, it might hurt, and no, she might not get the guy, but true love was worth fighting for. And friendship was the basis of every good marriage. Diane's words had brought a new perspective to Juliet's own view of marriage. What if the common denominator had been true friendship? A genuine like and respect for one another, combined with attraction. Love would blossom from friendship.

Which is exactly what had happened to her. So why couldn't it happen to Jake?

Juliet brushed her hair until it shined, added a light touch of makeup and picked out a fresh pair of jeans and a flowery, blue and yellow blouse that accented her eye color. Satisfied with her appearance, she filled out the application and headed for the door, determined to see this through.

It took her almost thirty minutes to drive to Jake's cabin, Juliet unwilling to drive fast on the back roads. It still seemed like too short a time. She sucked in a deep breath, trying to calm her nerves. It was one thing to decide to be bold, another to act on it. Nervous anticipation rippled across every nerve.

His truck was parked in front of the barn, as was his four-wheeler. There was no turning back now. She knocked on the screen door and waited.

Seconds later, Jake filled the doorway. "Juliet? What are you doing here?"

"Good morning to you, too." She attempted a smile but failed miserably.

"Forgive me. I'm just surprised to see you here. I thought you returned to Memphis."

"I did, but remember that I promised to help out at the Shakespeare festival this weekend, so I'm back."

"Nice of you to help out. It still doesn't explain why you're on my doorstep, but I'm sure you'll get around to that. Can I get you a cup of coffee?" After his last email, she was stunned at the offer.

Juliet was tempted, but she wanted to do this right. Not overwhelm Jake and send him running for the hills. Further than he already had, considering he'd been a recluse for a couple of years.

"No, thanks. I wanted to tell you to face to face, I'm sorry about what happened. What I did. You were right about me. I did decide to help you initially as a project." She winced as the last word slipped out. "And it was wrong." Juliet let out a deep breath. "I only wanted to help, but instead of being supportive and a good friend, I manipulated things for the out-come I desired, not considering what you wanted. I'm truly sorry." She winced at even saying the word.

"About that—"

She held up her hand when he started to speak. "I had only just come to the realization that love and family might not be God's plan for my life and that helping others might be. And then when I met you, my heart was filled with a need to comfort you and help you get past the grief holding you back from living life. I realized as we became friends and started working together that it was more than that. I wasn't helping you because you were a project, I was helping because I genuinely cared about you and I went about it in all the wrong way."

Jake let out a deep sigh and ran his hands through his hair. "Apology accepted. We were friends and I shouldn't have jumped to conclusions, even if they were partially right." His lips twitched, as if he were fighting back a smile. "Are you sure you don't want to stay for coffee?"

They'd come to a truce and there was no sense pushing him any harder. Time was on her side if Jake hired her as an APRN at the clinic. Whether they were friends or more depended on Jake, but no matter what, they'd always be friends. "No, thanks."

"You could have called to apologize."

"But then I couldn't have given you this," Juliet said, reaching into her handbag to retrieve the application. "I'm applying for the position of APRN at the clinic. Full-time. *Permanent.*"

Jake's eyes grew wide, the hint of a smile teasing his mouth. "What about the job in Memphis? I don't understand."

"I like working with you. I like Hollow Creek. I like the people I've gotten to know here. I want to come back. To stay—but I need a job."

Jake reached out to hand her back the application. "I don't need this," he said, shaking his head.

Juliet was crushed and did the best she could to hide the disappointment. Which was tough considering the tears threatening to spill over. It was time to cut and run. She'd figure out her next step away from Jake and his outright rejection. He really hated her for what she'd done, contrary to his apology.

As she tried to pull the application from his grasp, Jake held on. Juliet looked up at him, confused. Several seconds passed before he released his grip on he papers.

Juliet turned to leave. "Take care then, Jake." She stepped off the porch, eager to get away.

"You're hired," Jake called out, stopping her in her tracks.

She spun around, not sure she heard what she thought she heard. "What?"

"You're hired. I don't need an application because your information is already in the system and you already have the job." He smiled. A full smile as glorious as the sun shining down on them.

Joy overwhelmed her, the tears falling. She brushed them away and nodded. "Thank you. You won't regret it."

"I'm sure I won't. Welcome home, Juliet Walker."

Juliet spent the rest of Saturday trying to set up the house she had re-rented. It wasn't such a big town that the place had been rented in her three-day absence, something for which Juliet was relieved. She loved the old house; the gardens and trellis in the backyard, warm and welcoming. Inside, the place held history. Many nights she'd thought about the families who might have grown up here and imagined the sounds of laughing children.

It was like coming home.

Sunday morning arrived early, considering her late night. She pushed back the covers, basking in the glow of sunlight streaming through the bedroom window. Two cups of coffee later, she was dressed and ready to walk to church. It was yet another reason she loved the old house...it was walking distance from everything.

Juliet said hello to several people as they stopped to chat, many others simply waving, but all made her feel like she was a part of the community. But then, she treated quite a few patients or their children in the three weeks she'd been in town.

She slid into a seat toward the back of the sanctuary, enjoying the soft music coming from the front stage area. The praise team hadn't started yet and the instrumental strains soothed Juliet as she relaxed, peace filling her.

Someone slid in next to her and she looked up, a ready smile on her face. The greeting she was about to say died on her lips when she spotted Jake as he sat next to her.

After a few seconds, she recovered from the shock. "This is a pleasant surprise," she said, smiling. Juliet tried her best to tamp down the questions that sprung to her lips.

"I knew you'd be here." He winked. Taking her hand just as the praise team started to play, she fell silent. Not only because of a loss for words but also wanting to hear the song.

The two of them sat there, holding hands, singing, and being in the presence of God. *Together*. What did it all mean? It was hard to focus on the sermon, but Juliet forced herself to sit still. The time for questions would come after the service.

She still couldn't believe Jake was here. It was a testament to his brave heart. He was facing his fears and embracing the future in a way she hadn't expected. Hoped perhaps, but had stopped expecting.

Chapter Twenty-One

♥

I T WAS A PEACEFUL message and morning, one that filled Juliet's heart with joy. Of course, the man sitting next to her had a lot to do with the joy. "That was beautiful," she said, standing with the rest of the congregation as they prepared to leave.

"It was, and you are," he said, smiling down at her. "We need to talk."

His words set her heart racing, but this wasn't a good time. For the first time in a long time, she was tempted to chuck responsibility out the window. "I'm sorry," she answered, glancing down at her watch. "I've got to get to the festival. Remember, I'm working there today, and they'll be looking for me shortly."

Jake looked disappointed, but not upset. "I hadn't forgotten, but perhaps we can talk after the festival."

"About?" she asked, curiosity consuming her.

"I'll tell you later when we have more time. Do you think they could use another set of hands to help out?"

"Seriously? You're volunteering? You do realize it's in town and there will be a lot of kids and people." She couldn't believe what he was asking. Jake, the recluse, was offering to help out at a large gathering of people. *To be with her?* The very thought made her nervous and giddy all in the same space of seconds.

He shrugged. "I've managed worse. Try me."

"You're on. Let's go." Juliet pulled him by the hand that he had yet to let go of, as she led him out of the church. Several people must have had the same idea because there were several large groups headed to the town square.

"Hey, Dr. K., didn't take you for a Shakespearean kind of guy." Ryan Jenkins, one of her patients, clapped Jake on the back and fell in step next to him.

"Can't say as I was, but I'm willing to give it a try."

"I see you have a little encouragement in that department." Ryan chuckled. "Seems the womenfolk have that effect on us."

"Don't let him fool you. He offered, I didn't ask," Juliet joined in the teasing.

Ryan grinned. "The truth is out. You do realize once you start down this road, there's no going back."

"What road is that?" Jake asked, looking sweetly perplexed. It made Juliet love him all that much more.

"Pleasing the little woman."

Juliet almost choked on Ryan's words, worried about how Jake would take them.

"Oh, I think Juliet can hold her own, with or without me. I've seen her in action." So she needn't have worried. This was a new Jake, and even she was having a hard time figuring out what he would say next.

"He's right, but *with* sounds like more fun. I'll have to keep your manly words of wisdom in mind when I start dating someone." She grinned, shooting Jake a direct look, preferring to have a private conversation with him to clear the air.

"Oh, I thought..." Ryan shook his head, as if at a loss for words.

"You thought wrong. Friends. Just friends," Juliet quickly assured Ryan.

"Mighty chummy friends, if you ask me."

"We didn't," they both answered in unison.

Juliet pulled her hand away from his, the two walking side by side. Once they arrived at the town square, she quickly located Evelyn Star, the chairperson of the event.

"Hi, Evelyn. I'm here. And I brought you a recruit. You can put him to work wherever he's needed." She gave Jake a gentle shove in her direction, not letting him have an opportunity to change his mind.

"It's great to see you, Juliet. I'm so glad you made it. Good afternoon, Dr. K, it's a pleasure to see you here. I'm sure I can find you the perfect job." Evelyn beamed.

"Great." Jake gazed at her, a slight smile on his face.

"The kids are going to gather over by the wishing well that's set up for donations. You'll find crafts and game ideas. Feel free to get set up and organize,

Juliet. You'll have one other helper and about twenty kids, so be prepared."

Juliet was okay with being a leader and helping, especially if it meant she was doing good for others. "Don't worry, it'll be fine. Kids are easy once you break them into groups and find what they like to do by age range."

"You had a knack at the church social, so I will totally take your word on it." Evelyn laughed. "As to you, Dr. K, give me a minute to figure it out."

Juliet gazed up at him and smiled. "See you later, and then we can talk."

"Sounds like a plan," he answered, shooting her a wink. The talk wouldn't come soon enough, as far as she was concerned.

"Why don't you help Tommy make sure the seating is set up with plenty of room toward the front for people to lay down with blankets? You can help direct people as they arrive and keep the crowd under control. Can't have empty seats in the middle." Evelyn smiled and pointed him in the right direction.

"Sounds perfect. I like being in charge," Jake said.

"That's the truth," Juliet said, waving as she walked away, wanting to get in the last word.

An hour had passed, and more kids showed up. Luckily, so did Evelyn, because Juliet needed help. "Thank goodness you stopped by. Is there anyone you can spare? We have way more children than you expected."

"Sure thing," Evelyn said with a grin. "Hey, Jake," she hollered.

Juliet swung around to see Jake walking by close to where they stood. Talk about timing.

Jake changed directions and headed their way. "What's up?" he asked.

"Juliet and Cecilia look like they could use a hand. Any chance you can help them out?" Evelyn's broad smile gave her the suspicion the woman was up to something. But if it included Jake, Juliet was all in.

Grizzly bear or teddy bear—Juliet was all in.

"Sure thing," he said, his quick reply and ready smile showing his eagerness to comply. "Let me give this to Mark," he held up a pack of paper, "and then I'll be right back.

Evelyn leaned in closer as he walked away. "Don't let him get away."

"He's not going anywhere. I've already agreed to come back to the clinic, and he has to stay there until they find someone else."

"I wasn't talking about work."

"The jury's still out on that one, but rest assured, I'm working on it." Now that she understood the root of her feelings and understood that life was a work in progress, she was more than willing to go the distance to see what could come of things between them. And if it was God's plan for them to be together, they would be. And Juliet was more than willing to find out.

Jake returned and made his way over to where the kids played.

A game of chase was quickly arranged. "Newcomer is it. Run kids!" Juliet shouted. The children scattered in every direction, Juliet holding the hand of one little girl on one side and a little boy on the other. They were an easy target, and Jake headed straight for them, turning aside at the last minute.

Proof he was one of the good guys. Jake caught up to Johnny and tagged him. "You're it. Hope you're being careful with that arm," he added.

"I am, Dr. K. When we going fishing?" Johnny asked.

"Juliet held her breath and waited for Jake's answer.

"How about next weekend?" he said, ruffling the boy's hair.

"Awesome." Johnny took off running, trying to catch the next person.

Within the hour, all the children and been picked up by the parents and the park was almost a ghost town, other than a few people left to clean up. "Need help, Evelyn?" Jake asked when the woman joined them.

"No thanks. Plenty of folks signed on for cleanup. They consider it the easy part," she added, laughing.

"Okay, then. Wonderful event. What I saw of the play was incredible and it was surprising to see so much talent in our local county. Can't wait to see next year's event," Jake said, this time his comment surprising Juliet beyond belief. The man was talking about making this social change beyond today.

"I'm glad you enjoyed it. You two run along," Evelyn said as Juliet handed her several bags of kids' toys and games.

"That was exhausting, but fun." Juliet grinned. "Thank you for asking me to help."

"Thanks to both of you for everything you did. I love it when the town comes together to make these events a success," Evelyn said, walking away.

"Do you have enough energy left for a walk?" Jake asked, offering his arm in another surprise move.

"If you carry me," she teased. The truth was, she could be dead on her feet and she'd find a way to walk with Jake and finally find out what he wanted to talk about.

"That can be arranged." Jake made a move to do just that, not at all put off by the idea.

"I'm teasing," she said, grabbing his arm instead. "Lead on."

Jake walked her toward the wishing well. He stopped, turning to face her. "You came by to tell me some truths and apologize, and now it's my turn to do the same."

"You have—"

He held up his hand to stop her. "Let me finish. You came to me at a low point in my life. One that had been going on far too long. You challenged me to move past it all and start living again. I've done that, thanks to you. Your motives in the beginning might not have been entirely on the up and up, but they weren't misguided either. You once told me it was a tragedy not to use my God-given talents for doctoring, and you were right.

"It's also a tragedy not to use my God-given talent for loving. *You.* I know I pushed you away, but I was afraid of my feelings. And I felt guilty, as though I were betraying Sophia. I now know and understand that how fortunate I've been to have met two beautiful, and yet unique, women. God has blessed me with another chance at love and I would be honored if you'd give me a chance to prove how much I love you." Jake took her hand and held it to his lips, pressing a kiss against the warmth of her flesh.

Tears glazed her eyes, her mouth trembling.

She could tell Jake wanted to kiss her, but something was holding him back. Her? Was he waiting for permission? "I'd like that. In case you haven't noticed, I love you, too. I have for a long time; I just didn't want to admit it." It felt wonderful to let loose the words from her heart and to know they were well received.

Jake leaned forward, letting his mouth do the necessary talking. She wrapped her arms around his neck as if it were the most natural thing in the world. Like she was right where she belonged.

Epilogue

JULIET SAT ROCKING ON the front porch of the cabin. It was hard to believe almost a year had passed since she first met Jake and stayed here. But then, a full-time job at the clinic, a wedding, and now a baby on the way, had kept them busy. Jake's wedding proposal had come swiftly on the heels of his declaration of love. Like three weeks swift.

She smiled, remembering the hike they'd taken on one of the trails to their favorite overlook of the Smoky Mountains and the valleys below. Just as the sun was setting, he'd proposed. Romantic and beautiful. Exactly what she would have wanted the day she said yes.

God's plan had included Jake, marriage, and a family. All when it was the right time in her life. The wedding had been three weeks later. Jake was a man who moved mountains to get his way when he was determined, and he'd been determined the two of them would be settled by Christmas.

What they hadn't planned was a baby coming along so quickly. As spring rolled in, the warmer weather days increased, and so did her belly. Juliet rubbed her abdomen as their baby girl kicked, letting Mom know she wasn't enjoying the rocker. She hoped that would change when baby Rebecca Sophia Kensington made her appearance in four months, but for now, she quit rocking.

They were here for a vacation. Their first official one since finding a temporary doctor to take over the clinic in their absence. Although, it wasn't much of a vacation for Jake. He was determined to have Rebecca's room and an indoor bathroom added to the cabin for when they vacationed here. Their other home, of course, was the one Juliet had fallen in love with while renting the place in town. The one Jake had bought for her as a wedding present. The man was full of surprises and showed his love every way he could think of.

Juliet peered off into the distance as something caught her attention out of the corner of her eye. Down along the tree line she spotted a fox easing its way closer. She loved the wildlife out here in the woods, but the little fox who showed up the day after she met Jake would always hold a special place in her heart because Juliet was pretty sure that's when she'd fallen for the warm and kind-hearted man who he was.

"Jake," she called softly, not wanting to alarm the fox.

"What is it, darling? Do you need something?" he asked, standing in the doorway, a hammer in his hand.

"No, but thanks. I wanted to let you know the fox is here." She pointed toward the trees where she'd last spotted it.

He moved to stand next to her on the porch.

Juliet grabbed his arm. "I wonder if it's our special fox. The one you saved."

"You ask that every time a fox shows up, but I'm not sure there's any way to find out. They all look alike to me." He laughed.

"Look. It's her. I just know it is. I think we should name her Ginger." Juliet grinned up in excitement and pointed. The fox suddenly appeared from behind the wood pile and sat looking at them, before laying down, not at all afraid.

"It's a great name and I think you're right; it is her." He nodded, placing a hand on her shoulder.

"It's like she keeps coming back to thank you for saving her."

"Wouldn't surprise me. I do that every day with you. Give thanks for you saving me," he clarified, dropping a kiss on her mouth.

"We both had a lot to learn from each other. Once we got out of our own way, God was able to show us the right direction, the one that led us to each other." Juliet stood and stepped into Jake's arms, the two of them watching their fox in silent wonder.

What to read next?

If you enjoyed JULIET'S JOURNEY TO LOVE, be sure to check out

POPPY'S PATH TO LOVE AND RACHEL'S ROAD TO LOVE in the GREAT SMOKY MOUNTAIN GET-AWAYS series.

BONUS READ

Want to keep in touch with new releases and what's happening in the world of Elsie Davis?

Sign up for the monthly newsletter at Elsie Davis HEA (Happily-Ever-After) and enjoy DIGGING THE DRIVER (A Celebrity Corgi Romance) as a FREE BOOK!

The greatest compliment you could give an author is to leave a review in order to help other readers discover the same great stories you enjoyed. Amazon/Bookbub/Goodreads are all great places. Many thanks!!!

Another great way to keep in touch - *Follow Elsie Davis on FaceBook*

Also By Elsie Davis

Sweet, Clean and Wholesome Stories...with a Happily-Ever-After Guarantee!

Holidays in Hallbrook

(Sweet Romance Series for Holidays Throughout the Year)

Welcome to Hallbrook, New Hampshire. A small-town filled with the unexpected, lots of love, and of course, a beloved dog to ramp up the excitement.

Love & Order (Labor Day)

Love & Family (Thanksgiving)

Love & Peace (Christmas)

Love & Chocolate (Valentine's Day)

Love & Hope (Mother's Day)

Love & Liberty (Independence Day)

Love & Honor (Veteran's Day)

Love & Joy (Easter)

Love & Adventure (Father's Day)

Great Smoky Mountain Getaways

(Christian Inspirational – Women's Fiction Romances)

Juliet's Journey to Love

Poppy's Path to Love

Rachel's Road to Love

Taylor's Trek to Love – 2024

Crossroads Creek Cowboys

(Christian Inspirational Romances)

The Heart of a Cowboy

The Help of a Cowboy

The Return of a Cowboy

The Care of a Cowboy

Crestfield Inn Romances

If you like special kinds of soulmates, a splash of the supernatural, and wholesome relationships, you'll adore this sweet bit of fun filled with romance and mystery.

Turning Back Time

Turning Up Roses

Turning Down Pie

Celebrity Corgi Romance

(Standalone Sweet Romance)

If you like light mystery mixed in with your happily-ever-after, you'll enjoy this second-chance romance and the race to save an adorable Corgi.

Digging the Driver

Gold Coast Retrievers

(Sweet Romance)

Special Golden Retrievers help their humans solve mysteries, save lives, and even find love...

Defending Dakota

Trinity River

(Sweet Western Romance)

Ranchers and farmers depend on the Trinity River for water, but when a secret conglomerate starts buying up property by fair means or foul, it's time for the landowners of Tumble County to fight back—Texas style. But what they don't count on, is finding love in the process.

Back in the Rancher's Arms

Small Town, Big Secrets

Sundancer's Legacy – 9 Book series

Sundancer's Star

Coming Soon – 2024

Sundancer's Joy

Sundancer's Heart

Sundancer's Majesty

Sundancer's Miracle

Sundancer's Glory

Sundancer's Kiss

Sundancer's Moon

Sundancer's Splendor

About The Author

Elsie Davis is a *USA Today and International Best-selling Author* of over 25 sweet, clean, and wholesome romances, and a member of the ACFW. She discovered the world of Happily-Ever-After romance at the age of twelve when she began avidly reading Barbara Cartland, the Queen of Romance, and has been hooked ever since. After building her dream log home on top of a small mountain, she turned her attention to do what she loves most, writing. Elsie writes sweet Contemporary Romance and Contemporary Christian Romance from her heart...hoping to share a little love in a big world.

When she's not writing, she can be found birding, kayaking, camping, fishing, playing disc golf, and taking nature walks—hoping to spot wildlife. Basically, she loves all things outdoors, EXCEPT cold weather. She and her husband are avid Caribbean cruisers, but Elsie's favorite vacation was their cruise to Alaska. (In spite of the cold!) Indoors, she enjoys a toasty fire, and of course, a great romance with a guaranteed Happily-Ever-After.

https://www.elsiedavishea.com